How
Tía Lola
Came to
~~Visit~~ Stay

How
Tía Lola
Came to
~~Visit~~ Stay

Julia Alvarez

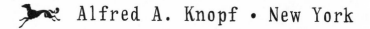 Alfred A. Knopf • New York

Library of Congress Cataloging-in-Publication Data
Alvarez, Julia.
How Tía Lola came to ~~visit~~ stay / Julia Alvarez.
p.   cm.
Summary: Ten-year-old Miguel learns to love his colorful aunt, Tía Lola, when she
comes to Vermont from the Dominican Republic to stay with his mother, his sister,
and him after his parents' divorce.
ISBN 0-375-90215-5 (lib. bdg.) — ISBN 0-375-80215-0 (trade)
[1. Aunts—Fiction. 2. Dominican Americans—Fiction. 3. Family life—Vermont—
Fiction. 4. Divorce—Fiction. 5. Vermont—Fiction.] I. Title.
PZ7.A48 Ho   2001
[Fic]—dc21   00-062932

Printed in the United States of America
April 2001
10 9 8 7 6 5 4 3 2 1

First Edition

For Susanna—
who could be Tía Lola
if she were from the islands
if she were into makeup & dressup
if she wore high heels
if she had jet-black hair
& a fake beauty mark above her upper lip
if she spoke Spanish
if she had been my aunt
instead of
my dear friend

and

(y)

Para mis queridas tías—
Tía Rosa y Tití y Tía Idalita
Tía Teolinda y Tía Laurita y Tía Josefina
Tía Ana y Tía Claudina y Tía Fofi y Tía Edí
Tía Anny y Tía Lulú y Tía Clara
Tía Carmenza y Tía Estela—
tantas tías queridas
que ayudaron a criarme
y me dieron con su amor
esperanza
y alegría

¡Gracias, tías!

Contents

How
Tía Lola
Came to
~~Visit~~ Stay

Chapter One

▼▼▼

Tía Lola Comes to Visit

"Why can't we just call her *Aunt* Lola?" Miguel asks his mother. Tomorrow their aunt is coming from the Dominican Republic to visit with them in their new home in Vermont. Tonight they are unpacking the last of the kitchen boxes before dinner.

"Because she doesn't know any English," his mother explains.

"*Tía* is the word for aunt in Spanish, right, Mami?" Juanita asks. When their mother's back is turned, Juanita beams Miguel a know-it-all smile.

Their mother is gazing sadly at a blue bowl she has just unpacked. "So you see, Miguel, if you call her Aunt, she won't know you're talking to her."

That's fine, Miguel thinks, I won't have much to say to her except "*¡Adiós!*" Goodbye! But he keeps his mouth shut. He knows why his mother is staring at the blue bowl, and he doesn't want to upset her in the middle of a memory.

"So, please, Miguel," his mother is saying, "just call her Tía Lola. Okay?"

Miguel kind of nods, kind of just jerks his head to get his hair out of his eyes. It can go either way.

It is the last day of January. Four weeks ago, during Christmas break, they moved from New York City into a farmhouse Mami rented from a Realtor by phone. Miguel and Juanita's parents are getting a divorce, and Mami has been hired to be a counselor in a small college in Vermont. Papi is a painter who sets up department store windows at night in the city.

Every morning, instead of walking to school as they used to do in New York City, Miguel and Juanita wait for the school bus by the mailbox. It is still dark when they board and drive down the dirt road, past their neighbor's sheep farm to town. It is again dark when they get home at the end of the day and let themselves into the chilly house. Mami does not like the idea of Miguel and Juanita being alone without an adult, and that in large part is why she has invited Tía Lola to come for a visit.

Why not ask Papi to come up and stay with them instead? Miguel wants to suggest. He doesn't really understand why his parents can't stay married even if they don't get along. After all, he doesn't get along great with his little sister, but his mother always says, "Juanita's your *familia*, Miguel!" Why can't she say the same thing to herself about Papi? But Miguel doesn't dare suggest this to her. These days, Mami bursts out crying at anything. When they first drove up to the old house with its peeling white paint, Mami's eyes filled with tears.

"It looks haunted," Juanita gasped.

"It looks like a dump," Miguel corrected his little sister. "Even Dracula wouldn't live here." But then, catching a glimpse of his mother's sad face, he added quickly, "So you don't have to worry about ghosts, Nita!"

His mother smiled through her tears, grateful to him for being a good sport.

After some of the boxes have been cleared away, the family sits down to eat dinner. They each get to pick the can they want to bring to the table: Juanita chooses SpaghettiOs, their mother chooses red beans, and Miguel chooses a can of Pringles. "Only this one night, so we can finish getting settled for Tía Lola," their mother explains about their peculiar dinner. Every night, she gets home so late from work, there is little time for unpacking and cooking. Mostly, they have been eating in town at Rudy's Restaurant. The friendly, red-cheeked owner, Rudy, has offered them a special deal.

"Welcome Wagon Special," he calls it. "Three meals for the price of one and you guys teach me some Spanish." But even Miguel is getting tired of pizza and hot dogs with french fries on the side.

"Thanks for a yummy dinner, Mami," Juanita is saying, as if their mother has cooked all the food and put it in cans with labels marked Goya and SpaghettiOs, then just now reheated the food in the microwave. She always sees the bright side of things. "Can I have some of those chips, Miguel?" she asks her brother.

"This is my can," Miguel reminds her.

"But you can share," his mother reminds him. "Pretend we're at the Chinese restaurant and we share all the plates."

"We're not Chinese," Miguel says. "We're Latinos." At his new school, he has told his class-mates the same thing. Back in New York, lots of other kids looked like him. Some people even thought he and his best friend, José, were brothers. But here in Vermont, his black hair and brown skin stand out. He feels so different from every-body. "Are you Indian?" one kid asks him, im-pressed. Another asks if his color wears out, like a tan. He hasn't made one friend in three weeks.

"I didn't say to pretend you're Chinese," his mother sighs, "just to pretend that you're at a Chinese restaurant...." She suddenly looks as if she is going to cry.

Miguel shoves his can of chips over to Juanita—anything to avoid his mother bursting into tears again. She is staring down at her bowl as if she had forgotten it was there underneath her food the whole time. From that blue bowl, Miguel's mother and father fed each other spoon-fuls of cake the day they got married. There is a picture of that moment in the white album in the box marked ALBUMS/ATTIC that their mother says they might unpack sometime later in the distant future maybe.

Juanita must have also noticed how sad Mami

looks. She begins asking questions about Tía
Lola because it makes their mother happy to talk
about her favorite aunt back on the island where
she was born. "How old is she, Mami?"

"Who?"

"Tía Lola, Mami, *Tía Lola que viene mañana*,"
Juanita says in Spanish. It also makes their mother
happy when they use Spanish words. *Tía* for
"aunt." *Mañana* for "tomorrow." Tía Lola who
comes tomorrow. "Is she real old?"

"Actually, nobody knows how old Tía Lola is.
She won't tell," their mother says. She is smiling
again. Her eyes have a faraway look. "She's so
young at heart, it doesn't matter. She'll be fun to
have around."

"Is she married?" Juanita asks. Mami has told
them they have tons of cousins back on the island, but are any of them Tía Lola's kids?

"I'm afraid Tía Lola never did get married,"
Mami sighs. "But, kids, do me a favor. Just don't
ask her about it, okay?"

"Why not?" Juanita wants to know.

"It's a sensitive issue," her mother explains.

Juanita is making her I-don't-understand-
this-math-problem face. "But why didn't she get
married?"

Miguel speaks up before his mother can answer. He doesn't know how the thought has popped into his head, but it suddenly pops out of his mouth before he can stop it. "She didn't get married so she wouldn't have to get divorced ever."

Mami blinks back tears. She stands up quickly and leaves the room.

Miguel studies the beans pictured on the outside of the can his mother has picked for dinner. One little bean has on a Mexican hat.

"You made Mami cry!" Juanita blubbers tearfully and follows their mother out of the room.

Miguel finds himself alone in a drafty kitchen with all the dirty bowls and plates to wash and the table to wipe. As he cleans up at the sink, he glances out the window at the frosty world outside. Up in the sky, the moon is just the tiniest silver sliver. It looks as if someone has gobbled up most of it and left behind only this bit of light for Miguel to see by.

For the first time since he heard the news, he is glad his aunt is arriving tomorrow. It might be nice to have a fourth person—who is still talking to him—in the house, even if her name is Tía Lola.

* * *

The next morning at the airport, Miguel's mother cannot find a parking space. "You kids, go in so we don't miss your aunt. I'll join you as soon as I find a spot."

"I'll help you," Miguel offers.

"Miguel, *amor*, how can you help me? You don't have a license. The cops'll take you in if they catch you driving," his mother teases.

As nervous as Miguel is feeling about his aunt's visit and his new school and their move to Vermont, he thinks he wouldn't mind spending the next year all by himself in jail.

"*Por favor*, honey, would you go inside with your sister and look for Tía Lola?" His mother's sweetened-up voice is like a handful of chocolate chips from the package in the closet. Impossible to resist.

"*¡Los quiero mucho!*" she calls out to both children as they clamber out of the car.

"Love you, too," Juanita calls back.

The crowd swarms around them in the small but busy terminal.

Juanita slips her hand into Miguel's. She looks scared, as if all that Spanish she has been showing off to their mother has just left on a plane to South America. "You think we'll recognize her?" she asks.

"We'll wait until somebody who looks like *she's* looking for *us* comes out of the plane," Miguel says. He sure wishes his mother would hurry up and find a parking spot.

Several businessmen rush by, checking their watches, as if they are already late for whatever they have come for. Behind them, a grandma puts down her shopping bag full of presents, and two little boys run forward and throw their arms around her. A young guy turns in a slow circle as if he has gotten off át the wrong stop. A girl hugs her boyfriend, who kisses her on the lips. Miguel looks away.

Where is this aunt of theirs?

The crowd disperses, and still their aunt is nowhere in sight. Miguel and Juanita go up to the counter and ask the lady working there to please page their aunt. "She doesn't know any English," Miguel explains, "only Spanish."

The woman in the blue suit has so many freckles, it looks as if someone has spilled a whole bag of them on her face. "I'm sorry, kids. I took a little Spanish back in high school, but that was ages ago. I'll tell you what. I'll let you page your aunt yourself."

"She'll do it." Miguel nudges his sister forward. Even though he is older, Juanita is the one who is always showing off her Spanish to their father and mother.

Juanita shakes her head. She looks scared. She looks about to cry.

"There's nothing to be scared of," Miguel encourages, as if he himself has paged his aunt every day of his life.

"That's right, sweetie," the woman agrees, nodding at Juanita. But Juanita won't budge. Then, turning to Miguel, the woman suggests, "Seeing as she's scared, why don't you do it instead?"

"I don't speak Spanish." It isn't technically a lie because he doesn't know enough to speak Spanish in public to a whole airport terminal.

"You do, too," Juanita sniffles. "He knows but he doesn't like to talk it," she explains to the airline lady.

"Just give it a try," the freckled lady says, opening a little gate so they can come behind the counter to an office on the other side. A man with a bald head and a tired face and earphones sits at a desk turning dials on a machine. The lady explains that the children need to page a lost aunt who does not speak any English.

"Come here, son." The man beckons to Miguel. "Speak right into this microphone. Testing, testing." He tries it out. The man adjusts some knobs and pushes his chair over so Miguel can stand beside him.

Miguel looks down at the microphone. He can feel his stomach getting queasy and his mind going blank. All he can remember of his Spanish is Tía Lola's name and the word for "hello."

"*Hola, Tía Lola,*" Miguel says into the microphone. Then, suddenly, the corny words his mother says every night when she tucks him into bed, the ones she has just called out when he and Juanita climbed out of the car, pop out. "*Te quiero mucho.*"

Juanita is looking at him, surprised. Miguel scowls back. "It's the only thing I remember," he mutters. With all the stuff popping out these days, he's going to have to get a brake for his mouth.

"I remember more!" Juanita boasts. She steps forward, her fears forgotten, and speaks into the microphone. *"Hola, Tía Lola,"* she says in a bright voice as if she is on TV announcing sunny weather tomorrow. *"Te esperamos por el mostrador."* She and Miguel will be waiting by the counter. *"Te quiero mucho,"* she closes, just as Miguel has done. I love you lots.

As Miguel and his sister walk out of the office, they hear a tremendous shout. It isn't a shout in Spanish, and it isn't a shout in English. It's a shout anyone anywhere would understand.

Someone is mighty pleased to see them.

On the other side of the counter stands their aunt Lola. You can't miss her! Her skin is the same soft brown color as theirs. Her black hair is piled up in a bun on her head with a pink hibiscus on top. She wears bright red lipstick and above her lips she has a big black beauty mark. On her colorful summer dress, parrots fly toward palm trees, and flowers look ready to burst from the fabric if they can only figure out how.

Behind their aunt, their mother is approaching in her hiking boots and navy-blue parka, her red hat and mittens. "Tía Lola!" she cries out. They hug and kiss and hug again. When Tía Lola pulls away, the beauty mark above her upper lip is gone!

"Those two," Tía Lola is saying in Spanish to Miguel's mother as she points to him and Juanita, "those two gave me my first welcome to this country. *¡Ay, Juanita! ¡Ay, Miguel!*" She spreads her arms for her niece and nephew. *"Los quiero mucho."*

It is a voice impossible to resist. Like three handfuls of chocolate chips from the package in the closet, a can of Pringles, and his favorite SpaghettiOs, all to himself. For the moment, Miguel forgets the recent move, his papi and friends left behind in New York. When Tía Lola wraps her arms around him, he hugs back, just as hard as he can.

Chapter Two

▼▼▼

Bienvenida, Tía Lola

Miguel cannot believe how much luggage his aunt has brought from the Dominican Republic!

Two big suitcases, covered in plastic wrap. *"Para más seguridad,"* Tía Lola explains. For more security. She raises her eyebrows as if the crown jewels are packed inside.

A box with a piñata, which Tía Lola says they should save for a special occasion.

A duffel bag full of gifts from their cousins, aunts, and uncles.

A tube with a rolled-up Dominican flag inside.

A flowered carpetbag with Tía Lola's *cositas*, her thises and thats.

Miguel looks at the pile of luggage, which he

has helped unload from the car. "How long did you say you were staying, Tía Lola?" he asks.

"*¿Qué dice?*" Tía Lola wants to know what Miguel has asked.

Miguel shakes his head and picks up a bag. He starts the long trek up the stairs to the room they have fixed up for his aunt.

The next day, Tía Lola is still unpacking.

"*No sabía que traer,*" she explains. She didn't know what to bring, so she brought a little of everything.

First, Tía Lola unpacks a small case she has carried by hand. It is full of makeup and rollers, earrings and several jars with odd ingredients, which Mami says are probably potions. Tucked at the bottom is a bottle of *Agua de Florida*, which Tía Lola sprinkles around the room.

"Why'd she do that?" Miguel asks his mother.

"It's good-luck water," Mami explains. Tía Lola is something of a *santera*. "It's like a doctor who works with magic instead of medicine."

"Can I tell the kids in school?" Juanita asks. Her face is full of excitement as if she has just learned she has a relative who came over on the *Mayflower*.

"Please, Mami, tell her not to," Miguel pleads. All he needs is for his new classmates to find out he has a nut case for a relative.

Tía Lola unpacks her bright summer dresses and her black hat with a veil. She unpacks a half-dozen pairs of high heels to match all the different colors of her outfits, and a dozen bright *pañuelos* to wrap around her head like a turban when she is working her magic. Her closet looks like a midsummer flower garden.

She unpacks her maracas and *tambor* to make music in case there is a fiesta. She puts on her castanets and clacks around the room, stomping her feet as if she is throwing a tantrum. Their mother and Juanita join in, acting goofy. "Isn't she fun?" his mother keeps asking Miguel.

Tía Lola unpacks bags of *café* and brown sugar, which go up on the kitchen shelves. Her spices—*hierbabuena, orégano, anís, hojas de guanabana, ajíes*—hang from the rafters. She also brings along her *guayo* to grate *yuca* and her *burén* to shape it into flat, round *casave* loaves. The *guayo* looks like an oversized grater and the *burén* like a large, smooth stone. Tía Lola's *verdura* seeds are put in a pot to germinate.

"¡Ay, *qué bueno!*" Miguel's mother claps her hands. "We'll have real Dominican cooking in Vermont! We'll have to invite Rudy over."

She is helping Tía Lola drape her mantilla across a window. It looks like a beautiful black spiderweb with a bright red rose pinned at the center. As they work, they dance to one of Tía Lola's merengues on the stereo. Juanita follows along, moving her hips, one-two, one-two, one-two.

"Isn't she fun?" their mother keeps asking.

"I guess," Miguel mutters, and then, because his mother is looking straight at him, he adds, "She's *lots* of fun, Mami."

Miguel has to admit there is one totally fun thing about Tía Lola.

She tells great stories.

None of Tía Lola's stories sound exactly true, but Miguel doesn't care. While he listens, he feels as if he isn't in Vermont at all, but in a magical world where anything can happen. In fact, what is most magical is how, even though in his daily conversations with Tía Lola, Miguel sometimes doesn't understand Tía Lola's Spanish, still, when she tells stories, Miguel seems to understand every word.

"*Había una vez...*," Tía Lola begins. Once upon a time...And Miguel feels a secret self, different from his normal everyday self, rising up like steam from a boiling kettle into the air and disappearing inside Tía Lola's stories.

Every night, Tía Lola gathers Miguel and Juanita in her bedroom. While their mother takes some time to herself or makes phone calls or continues unpacking boxes still stacked in the attic, Tía Lola tells them all about their large and exciting Dominican family.

She tells about their uncle with six fingers who can do anything with his hands, and about their great-grandmother who could read the future from looking at the stains in a coffee cup, and about their cousin who once befriended a *ciguapa* with *pastelitos*, little fritters filled with ground meat. As for *ciguapas*, they are beautiful, mysterious creatures who come out at night, but no one can ever catch them. They have a special secret. The *cigua-pas'* feet are on backward, so they leave footprints in the opposite direction of where they are going!

The next weekend, since he has no friends here and nothing better to do, Miguel tries out that trick in the snow. The footprints look hay-wire and messy, like someone stumbling around. But they do not look like *ciguapa* footprints.

One afternoon, two of Miguel's classmates show up at the front door. In the car, the mother of one of the boys waits, peering up at the old, gabled house. The boys are collecting money for the town's Little League team. Come spring, they will need equipment and uniforms.

"Wow!" Miguel says. "I'd really like to be on that team."

"You should try out," one of the boys says. The taller one's name is Dean. He has bright blue eyes that Miguel's father would call ultra-marine and a wide grin his mother would call trouble with a capital T.

As the boys stand in the mudroom talking, Tía Lola walks by in her spiked heels and white turban, holding up a plate of smoking embers.

She has already cleansed the basement and is on her way upstairs. She wants to cast out any bad spirits and attract good spirits and magical *ciguapas* from the island. The boys' mouths drop open.

"Wh-wh-who's that?" the smaller boy, Sam, asks. His fine blond hair stands on end naturally from electricity. But now he looks as if he has just had a terrible fright.

Miguel turns his head and looks, then shrugs as if no one is there. As the boys hurry down the front steps, Miguel hears Dean say, "I bet it was a ghost. My mom says this old house is haunted."

Miguel shuts the door and leans against it, his face pale as if he *has* seen a ghost. When he looks up, Tía Lola is looking back at him.

That night, a snowstorm blows in. When Miguel glances out the window the next morning, flakes are still falling in the light by the front porch. Downstairs, Tía Lola is not at breakfast.

"Good news," Juanita says as Miguel sits down. "No school today!"

"I do have to go to work," their mother

reminds them. "I'm so glad Tía Lola is here so I don't have to worry about you. Where is she anyhow?" Their mother glances up at the clock. "She's usually up at this hour. She seemed a little sad last night."

"She wouldn't tell us a story," Miguel admits.

"Did you hurt her feelings?" Since she is a psychologist, their mother always guesses everything that happens has to do with people's feelings.

"How could I hurt her feelings?" Miguel says, trying not to sound annoyed at his mother. *Her* feelings are awfully sensitive these days. "I don't know enough Spanish to hurt Tía Lola's feelings."

"Tía Lola is a special person," Miguel's mother observes. "She can tell the secret feelings in a person's heart." Miguel's mother gives him a look as if *she* can tell what is in his heart.

The truth is Miguel has mixed feelings about having Tía Lola around. She is fun, but he sure doesn't think having her here will improve his chances of making new friends. Why can't Tía Lola act more like his teacher, Mrs. Prouty, who speaks without moving her jaw and is so proper that she says, "Pardon me" *before* she sneezes. Or like farmer Becky, their shy next-door neighbor, who dresses in a white pullover sweater as if she wants to blend in with the sheep she shears and tends. Or even like their mother's new friend, Stargazer, who, although she wears fanciful, long skirts and dangly earrings, speaks in a soft voice in order not to stir up negative energies.

"You have to love people for who they are," his mother is saying, "then they will become all they can be."

That sounds like a riddle, but it makes sense. When Miguel first started playing baseball, Papi would always say, "Great swing, Miguel," or "Nice try," even when Miguel missed the ball. Over time, his playing actually got better because of Papi's encouragement.

"Remember," his mother continues, "Tía Lola might be a little homesick. She needs to feel really welcomed."

Miguel looks down at his cereal. Today he has gotten the blue bowl. He is sorry that he has made Tía Lola feel unwelcomed. He knows what that feels like. At school, an older kid in his class named Mort has nicknamed him Gooseman, because that's what Miguel's last name, Guzmán,

sounds like in English. Now other kids are calling out, "Quack, quack!" whenever they pass
him in the hall. Maybe they are trying to be
funny, but it makes him feel embarrassed and
unwelcomed.

"What's the word for welcome in Spanish?"
Miguel asks his mother.

"*Bienvenido* for a man, *bienvenida* for a
woman." His mother spells out the words. "Why
do you ask?"

"I've got a great idea. Nita, I'll need your
help."

Juanita nods. She loves to be included in her
brother's Great Ideas. She doesn't even have to
know what they are ahead of time.

The snow is deep, almost to his knees. Miguel
trudges down to the back field, keeping close to
the fence line. The sun has broken through the
clouds. All around him, the field is fresh and
unspoiled by footprints and sparkling with dia-
monds of light.

He starts by walking in a straight line, kick-
ing the snow to either side. Then he walks in a
half circle, out and back to the straight line, and

then out and back again. Every step of the way, he has to imagine what each mark will look like from the house.

He thinks of his father in New York. Although he works setting up department store windows at night, Papi's real love is painting. Today, Miguel feels the closest he has felt to his father since his mother and Juanita and he moved to Vermont. He is an artist like his father, but working on a larger canvas. He is trying to create something that will have the same result: making somebody happy.

At one point, he glances up, and he thinks he sees his little sister waving. It is her job to keep Tía Lola from looking out the windows.

The sun is right above his head when Miguel is done.

Inside, the house smells of something delicious baking in the oven. Tía Lola has prepared a special pizza with lots of cheese and black beans and *salchichón*, a tasty sausage that she has brought from the island.

"*Pizza dominicana*," Tía Lola calls it. "*Buen provecho*," she adds. It is what she always says before they eat. Their mom has told them it is sort of like wishing somebody a happy meal.

"Tía Lola's got to teach Rudy how to make this," Miguel says to his sister as Tía Lola serves him a third slice. "Pizza Tía Lola," he renames it in honor of his aunt.

When they have finished eating, Miguel announces there is a surprise for his aunt in the back field.

"*¿Para mí?*" Tía Lola says, pointing to herself.

Miguel can see the color coming back into her cheeks, the sparkle in her eyes. The beauty mark that was above her upper lip on the right side is now on the left side. Tía Lola tends to forget little things like that. It winks like a star.

Miguel leads the way up the stairs to the landing. They line up at the big picture window and look out at the snowy fields where large letters spell out *¡Bienvenida, Tía Lola!*

Tía Lola claps her hands and hugs Miguel.

"Who says I did it?" Miguel asks.

Juanita and Tía Lola look at him, surprised.

Miguel points to the tail on the *a* of LOLA. Tracks head toward the letters instead of away from them. Maybe the *ciguapas* have followed Tía Lola to Vermont.

"¡*Ay, Miguelito!*" Tía Lola kisses and hugs him all over again. "*Tú eres tan divertido.*"

"You're fun, too," Miguel says. This time he means it.

Chapter Three

▼▼▼

Top-Secret

At school, Miguel starts hanging out with Dean and Sam at recess. Almost every day, they practice pitching and catching in the gym. Miguel wants to be ready for spring tryouts for the town's Little League baseball team.

Dean and Sam have never brought up the incident with the ghost in the white turban. But Miguel has noticed they are none too eager to come over to his house after school or during weekends, which is just as well. How can he explain Tía Lola to them?

Once, as they are dressing for gym, Dean asks Miguel if living in the old Charlebois house is, like, well, maybe a little spooky? "At night," he adds, as if he doesn't want to be thought a scaredy-cat for asking.

"What do you mean?" Miguel stalls for time.

"He means, like, are there ghosts there?" Sam asks.

"Funny things happen," Miguel admits, trying to keep his fingers crossed as he puts on his sweat socks. "But I've learned not to pay attention to them."

Dean and Sam nod solemnly. Miguel can see a new respect in their eyes. They think he is brave for living in a haunted house with a real ghost. They don't know how real she is, Miguel thinks to himself.

This is how Tía Lola becomes top-secret.

It is hard to believe Tía Lola can be kept a secret. She is full of life. She is full of laughter. She is full of stories. And she is full of noise.

Some nights after supper, Tía Lola gives Juanita and Mami dance lessons. They move across the living room, stomping their feet and snapping their fingers, or shaking maracas and swaying their hips to the music of Fernandito Villalona and Juan Luís Guerra and Rafael Solano.

"If only Tía Lola could stay...," Mami says wistfully as she sits on Miguel's bed one night.

Under his blankets, Miguel crosses his fingers. "You said it was just a visit," he reminds his mother.

How can Tía Lola stay? She is not willing to learn English.

"Just learn a little bit," Juanita tries to convince her. "*Un poquito, Tía Lola.*"

"*¿Por qué?*" Tía Lola asks. There is no reason for it. She is just here for a visit. She can get along just fine without English.

"But nobody around here speaks Spanish," Juanita reminds her.

"*¡Qué pena!*" Tía Lola is shaking her head. What a pity! If the Americans are so smart, how come they haven't figured out that Spanish is easier than English? she wonders.

Miguel rolls his eyes. "Easier for whom?" he mutters.

"*¿Qué dice?*" Tía Lola wants to know what Miguel has said.

"*Nada, nada,*" Miguel replies. After all, he doesn't really want to hurt his aunt's feelings again. Besides, as long as Tía Lola doesn't know English, she won't venture out on her own. She can be kept a secret.

* * *

There is only one problem with a top-secret aunt.
A big-mouthed little sister in the second grade.

"I need to talk to you, Nita," Miguel tells his little sister one day after school. He always uses her nickname when he wants a favor from her. He has come into her bedroom and closed the door. He puts on his serious older-brother face, and speaks in a quiet, concerned voice. "Tía Lola might be sent back unless we're very careful."

Juanita's mouth drops open. "But who'll take care of me during the day till Mami comes home?"

Miguel grins. "I will."

Juanita looks worried. "Why would Tía Lola have to go back? She's part of our family." Juanita's bottom lip quivers. For a moment, Miguel is not sure he can go through with it.

"She's been here one whole month. People are only allowed to visit for twenty-one days."

"Let's tell Mami," Juanita says, jumping up out of her bed.

"Are you crazy?" Miguel says, yanking her back by the arm. "You know how worried and sad

Mami was before Tía Lola came? You want her to start worrying again?"

Juanita shakes her head no.

"We've just got to keep Tía Lola top-secret. You can't mention her in school, okay?"

Juanita nods slowly.

"If our friends come to the door, tell her to hide."

Juanita starts to nod, but suddenly her mouth drops open. She claps a hand over it.

"What?" Miguel wants to know. "You better tell me," he pleads with his sister. "Or else!"

"I can't," his sister says. "It's a secret." And before Miguel can catch her to sit on her and make her tell, Juanita runs out of her room and down the stairs.

Soon there is a second problem with a top-secret aunt.

Rudy begins his Spanish lessons.

Mondays, when his restaurant is closed, Rudy drives over in his old red pickup. "Almost as old as me," he likes to joke, patting it, as if the pickup were a barn animal. Rudy is tall and big-shouldered, with rumpled gray hair and thick eyebrows and red cheeks. He looks like someone who has lived in the Old West, but has retired to modern times in Vermont. When his wife died five years ago, he opened up a restaurant. "I love eating, but I hate eating alone," he tells his diners. He is always giving discounts and coming out of the kitchen in a white apron, holding a big pot of something he has just "invented" for everyone to try out.

The first night he steps into the Guzmán house, he smells the mouth-watering odors wafting from the kitchen. "Wow!" he says. "Smells like heaven in here."

Tía Lola comes into the room bearing a tray of *pastelitos*. She is wearing her palm-tree dress and a pink flower in her hair. "Looks like heaven!" Rudy adds, reaching for one of the fried, spiced treats she is offering him. Rudy is not shy. He eats seven of them.

From that moment on, the Spanish lessons turn into cooking lessons followed by a cup of espresso and a merengue dance lesson to top off the evening. Sometimes, Tía Lola throws in a little Spanish vocabulary between servings of whatever she has made that night.

"*Arroz con habichuelas,*" Tía Lola pronounces. That is the name of the rice and beans she is piling on Rudy's plate. "*Con un poquito de bacalao.*" With a little codfish.

"Sweetheart, honey," Rudy says, between mouthfuls, "I don't care what it's called. This is *magnificat!*" Rudy was an altar boy when he was Miguel's age, and Mami says that sometimes Rudy's Spanish sounds a lot like Latin. "Lola, I just love your cooking! *Adoremus! Adoremus!*"

"He's not learning much Spanish," Mami complains one night after Rudy has left.

"*¿Qué importa?*" Tía Lola says. What does it matter? Monday nights prove her point. You don't have to speak the same language to have fun with other people.

Some nights, when the dance lesson begins, Rudy pulls Miguel to his feet from the table. "*Venite, venite,*" he urges in his mangled Spanish. Miguel doesn't dare refuse. He has found out from Dean and Sam that, in addition to running a restaurant, Rudy is the coach for the Little League team. By the time practice begins, when Rudy might say something to Miguel's friends about his top-secret aunt, Tía Lola will hopefully be gone.

"This is just a visit," Miguel keeps reminding

himself as he shakes the two maracas in his hands.

It is the first of March, and Miguel has already started his countdown. In thirty days, seven hours, and twelve minutes, it will be exactly midnight, and the day of his birthday. Back in the city, he has always thought of his birthday as a spring birthday. But here in Vermont, spring never arrives until late in April. "If we're lucky," one of their neighbors, farmer Tom, has explained to him. "Makes for a long winter, I admit, but it keeps the flatlanders away." Miguel doesn't need to ask what a flatlander is. The look on Tom's face says he doesn't think very highly of them.

But even if spring is over a month away, there are hopeful signs. On weekend rides in the countryside, Miguel can see steam rising out of the sugar houses. When the family sits down to supper, there is just a tinge of light in the evening sky.

At the supper table one night, their mother asks Miguel and Juanita what happened that day in school. Then she asks Tía Lola what happened that day at home.

Tía Lola tells them that a man in a brown suit came to the door. But because the man was not El Rudy and Tía Lola has been told not to let in any strangers, she waved at him to go away.

"¡Ay, no!" Miguel's mother says. "That must have been the UPS guy. I'm expecting something...." She glances over at Miguel, and then back at Tía Lola, raising her eyebrows slightly.

Miguel sees a secret look traveling between his aunt and his mother.

"I'm expecting something, too," he says, in case anybody should be getting forgetful at this important time of year. His birthday is coming up in ten days, five hours, and thirty-three minutes.

"¡Ay, Dios mío!" his mother says, as if she just now remembered it.

"How you doing, tiguerito?" His father is on the phone. It is Saturday morning. In five more days, fourteen hours, and fifteen minutes, it will be Miguel's birthday. "What you planning for the big day?"

"Nothing much," Miguel replies. He feels

sad. This will be his first birthday without his father. No matter how special it is, it won't be special enough.

"Have you thought about what you want?"

Of course he has. More than anything, he wants his parents to be together. But he can't say that. He has already mentioned a few things to his mom: a new bat; a baseball signed by Sammy Sosa, who also came from the Dominican Republic, like Miguel's parents; Rollerblades; a visit from his best friend, José, once the weather gets nice. "One other thing," he tells his dad, lowering his voice. "I wish Tía Lola...I mean, she was supposed to come for a visit...and she's still here...and she won't even try to learn English...."

"Is that so? Maybe it's good to have your aunt around so you have to practice your Spanish."

"But the kids at school already think I'm different enough," Miguel explains. He is surprised that he is telling his father this much. "They can't even pronounce my last name!"

His father has gone very quiet on the other end. "*Mi'jo*," he finally says, "you should be proud of who you are. Proud of your Tía Lola. Proud of yourself."

It is Miguel's turn to be quiet. He knows his

father is right, but he can't help feeling what he feels.

"I know sometimes it's hard," his father is saying softly. "You'll grow into that pride the older you get. *Te quiero mucho*," he adds. "Don't forget."

For the next few days, the secret look that has been traveling between Tía Lola and Miguel's mother, and then Juanita, suddenly finds its way to Miguel's friends.

In the gym, Miguel comes upon Dean and Sam whispering. They stop the minute they see him.

"What's up?" he asks.

"Top-secret!" they chime in together, and then burst out laughing. Miguel doesn't know what they are laughing about. He feels uncomfortable, but he laughs along with them.

Friday morning, when Miguel comes downstairs, his mother is already eating her breakfast.

"*Buenos días*, Miguel," she says, looking up and frowning. "You're going to wear *that* to school today?" She stares at his Yankees sweat-shirt as if it has a bad smell to it.

"It's my favorite shirt," he reminds her. Just last Christmas, his father gave it to him. A few days later, his parents sat him and Juanita down and told them about the divorce.

Juanita walks into the kitchen. "Mami, where's my book bag? Oh, hi, Miguel. I thought I left it in the mudroom."

IT'S MY BIRTHDAY!!! Miguel feels like screaming.

Tía Lola has been outside feeding the birds. The minute she enters the room and sees Miguel, she throws her arms around him and gives him ten kisses, one for each year since he was born. Then she adds a couple more, which she calls his *ñapa.*

His mother stares pointedly at Tía Lola, the way she does when she wants to remind her of something without saying it out loud. "That's right, big boy," she says, play-punching him in the arm, "you're in the double digits now. Gotta run," his mother adds, glancing at her watch. "Staff meeting." She rolls her eyes.

"Guess I'll be catching the school bus today, the thirty-first of March, the anniversary of my first decade on planet Earth," Miguel says. If he can make his birthday sound important, maybe he'll get presents and lots of attention. Maybe he'll get a ride to school from his mami instead of having to ride the bus on his birthday.

"We'll celebrate later. Promise!" his mother calls as she heads out the door with her coat half off, half on.

All morning at school, Miguel feels gloomy. His friends are acting funny. No one wishes him "Happy birthday," though he has been dropping hints for the last few weeks.

"Want to hang out after school?" Miguel asks Dean as they head back for their classroom after recess.

"Can't today," Dean explains. "My mom's, um, picking me up early. Got...uh...uh... uh...a dentist appointment."

"I got...uh...a dentist appointment, too," Sam says when Miguel turns to him.

Nice friends, Miguel thinks. José would have hung out with him on his birthday instead of going to some stupid dentist. Maybe these new friends are not real friends, after all.

Miguel grows even gloomier as the day wears on.

That afternoon, Miguel comes out of school, head bowed, dragging his feet. His friends have run off early. The school bus is gone. Just as well, he would rather walk home than ride the noisy bus with his sister and her friends on his birthday.

When he looks up, he can't believe his eyes!

Just ahead stands his father in his jeans and leather jacket, holding Juanita's hand, a great big smile on his face. "Happy birthday, *tiguerito!*" he calls out.

Miguel drops his book bag and runs into his father's arms. This is the best birthday present ever. He hugs his father and then holds on a little longer while his moist eyes dry up.

"*¡Cóntrale!* It's cold here!" His father stomps his feet on the ground as if he, too, were taking dance lessons from Tía Lola.

They get in the rented car his father has driven from New York, and Juanita and Miguel give their father directions. It takes forever to get home. They pass farmhouses and rumbly bridges and fields with brown patches breaking through the snow. Their father keeps taking the wrong turn. As he drives, he tries playing an old game they used to play in New York. "What color is that?" he'd ask, pointing to something, and Miguel and Juanita have to name off the color from their father's oil paints. ("Cadmium yellow, raw umber, cobalt blue with a dab of titanium white?") But everything he points to here is gray, gray, gray.

When they finally pull up at the house, Miguel's mother's car is already in the drive, as is Rudy's red pickup.

As Miguel steps in the door, Sam and Dean spring out from behind the couch. "Surprise!" they shout. The table is piled high with gifts. Just above it hangs the parrot piñata Tía Lola has brought with her. Rudy is standing by, holding a hammer. He must have just finished putting it up.

Suddenly, Miguel understands everything. He is about to thank everybody when he hears one last shout coming from the kitchen. Before he can turn around and hide, his top-secret aunt walks in with a big cake in the shape of a baseball, showing off her one word of English. "Sooprise! Sooprise!"

Then everyone sings "Happy Birthday"—
in Spanish!

"We sort of rehearsed before you came," Sam
explains. "Your aunt taught us."

"I've never had a ghost for a teacher before!"
Dean adds, poking Miguel in the side.

Miguel feels his face getting red. But when
his friend bursts out laughing, Miguel cannot
help smiling.

He looks over at his father, who smiles back
at him. It's true what Papi has said. Miguel is ten
years old today and already feeling ten times
prouder of being who he is.

Chapter Four
▼▼▼

Lucky Love

Spring has arrived! There is no keeping Tía Lola indoors. She puts on her bright flowered dress and her high-heel *tacones*. She ties her yellow scarf around her neck, buttons up her heavy *suéter*, and sets out to meet the neighbors.

"Tía Lola!" Juanita and Miguel run after her. "*¡Tú no sabes hablar inglés!*" Someone has to remind their aunt that she doesn't know how to speak English.

"I ehspeak Eengleesh," Tía Lola replies, tossing the ends of the scarf over her shoulder as if to say, that is that. She always seems more determined when she wears that yellow scarf. "*Mi buena suerte*," she calls it. Her good-luck scarf.

* * *

They stop at the sheep farm next door. Tom is out cutting wood by the barn. "Howdy there, neighbors. Is this your aunt you told me about?" he asks Juanita.

Juanita nods. "Her name's Tía Lola. Actually, *tía* means 'aunt,' so you can't really call her that."

"How about Lady Lola?" Tom suggests.

"*Encantada,*" Tía Lola says, handing Tom her hand as if they were in the court of Queen Isabella, not in a stinky barnyard. But the real surprise is how the gruff farmer in his bib overalls and full red beard bows like a knight and kisses Tía Lola's hand.

"Enchanted, as well," he pronounces.

"Hey, Becky, hon," he calls over his shoulder. Blond, shy Becky, who can lift a bale as well as any man, comes out from the barn. She is carrying a small, bawling lamb.

"*¡Ay! ¡Qué cosita más mona!*" Tía Lola exclaims. What a cute little thing! Soon she has tied her yellow scarf around the lamb's neck.

"She is pretty, isn't she?" Becky smiles fondly at the lamb in Tía Lola's arms. "But she'll slobber all over your scarf if you don't take it off."

"*Mi buena suerte,*" Tía Lola explains. Her good-luck scarf.

"I've got a good-luck charm, too," Becky says. "Except it isn't a scarf but my 4-H bandanna."

Miguel has never heard Becky say this many words in the four months they have known her. All trace of shyness is gone as she chats along in English. Tía Lola nods and chats right back in Spanish. The two women aren't speaking the same language and yet they seem to understand each other perfectly!

Maybe her scarf *is* lucky? Maybe Tía Lola can work magic?

After the visit to the sheep farm, Miguel and Juanita and Tía Lola continue down the road. All around them, the fields are the pale green haze of new growth. The sky above them is a rich blue. If Papi were along, he would be pointing left and right. "What color is that?" Viridian-green hills, pale violet buds, and a tumble of titanium-white clouds in the cerulean-blue sky!

Tía Lola smiles at the weather vanes pointing south; she whistles at the swallows darting in and out of the barns; she waves at the farm woman cleaning out her garden, who waves back with her rake.

In town, they stop at Rudy's Restaurant. "*¡Hola!*" Tía Lola greets everyone as she walks in the door. Farmers in work clothes and professors from the college, grading papers, and teenagers with purple hair grin at the friendly woman. Little babies sitting in high chairs reach out their hands, motioning for Tía Lola to carry them. Only one customer, a sour-looking old man in a uniform, sitting at a corner table, glowers at Tía Lola as if her friendliness were a public disturbance.

Rudy comes out of the kitchen, shaking his head. He looks weary, and his smile is brief.

"I've been having a heck of a day," he confesses, nodding over their shoulders at the scowling man in the corner. It seems the old man has ordered huevos rancheros but keeps sending them back to the kitchen. Rudy has counted three returned orders. "He says they're not *real* huevos rancheros. That Colonel Charlebois is a royal pain in the— How do you say this in Spanish?" Rudy asks Tía Lola, slapping his backside.

Miguel begins to translate, but Tía Lola has already understood! "*Eso es el fundillo,*" she says, slapping her own *fundillo*. As for huevos rancheros, she has a special recipe that can turn the scowl on that *viejo*'s face into a boyish smile.

"Nothing short of magic is going to turn that old sourpuss around," Rudy grumbles as he heads back into the kitchen with Tía Lola to give huevos rancheros a fourth try.

Miguel sits at the counter, observing the old man. Colonel Charlebois...Colonel Charlebois... The name sounds familiar. Isn't that the name of the owner of their farmhouse? The Realtor said Colonel Charlebois had retired from the army years ago and moved back to the farm country where generations of his family had lived. But he had finally decided to rent out the old homestead and buy a place in town because of his bad arthritis. From their neighbors, Miguel has heard that Colonel Charlebois has turned into something of an oddball living all by himself. He insists on wearing his full-dress uniform and marching down the street as if he were inspecting the troops back in World War II.

The doors from the kitchen swing open. Tía Lola, bearing a plate of eggs covered with tomato sauce, onions, and peppers and followed by a worried-looking Rudy, heads for the corner table.

"*Buen provecho,*" Tía Lola says, setting the plate down in front of the old man. The old man nods as if he understands that Tía Lola has just wished him a happy meal. Then he puts a forkful in his mouth. It seems the whole room is holding its breath.

"These are the best darn huevos rancheros I've had north or south of the Rio Grande," the old man growls.

When the colonel has wiped the plate clean, Tía Lola asks him, "*¿Quiere más?*"

"That means, *Do you want more?*" Miguel calls from his perch on the stool.

"Of course that's what it means!" Colonel Charlebois barks. "I didn't travel all over the face of creation with the United States Army for nothing. And of course I want more! *Por favor,*" he adds, smiling up at Tía Lola.

Rudy is shaking his head as he follows Tía Lola back into the kitchen. "Magic, pure magic," he mutters.

By the time they get home that afternoon, Tía Lola has made a dozen new friends.

Miguel is astonished. He is not shy, but still,

after four months of living in Vermont, he has only two friends, Sam and Dean. Many of his classmates are friendly, but he can't really call them friends. Sometimes he sits with them in the lunchroom. But after exchanging complaints about how much homework Mrs. Prouty has given them or talking about the upcoming baseball tryouts, he doesn't know what else to say. At least some of them have stopped calling him Gooseman or making duck sounds when he walks down the hall.

There is only one conclusion that Miguel can come to. Rudy is right. His aunt is working magic on everybody. Miguel has never forgotten his mother's remark that Tía Lola is something of a *santera.*

"What exactly does a *santera* do?" he asks his mother that night.

"*Santeras* practice a religion called *santería,*" his mother explains.

"That explains a lot, Mami!" Miguel crosses his arms. "Okay, just tell me. Can Tía Lola help me get an A in my math exam? Can she help me make the team?"

His mother laughs and puts her arms around him. "Miguel, *amor,* your mother can tell you

how to do that." She pats his butt. "Apply your
~~fundillo to the seat of your chair and you'll get an~~
A if you study hard. As for making the team, eat
more of Tía Lola's cooking. I've asked Tía Lola
to make you some good Dominican food. Pizzas
and Pringles are not the most nutritious meals
for a budding major leaguer."

"Very funny," Miguel growls. Sometimes he
feels as cranky as Colonel Charlebois when his
mother teases him too much.

The next day in school, Miguel opens his lunchbox and finds four meatball-looking things
wrapped in tinfoil next to his can of Pringles. He
is about to toss them when Mort says, "What you
got there, Gooseman?"

Mort is a farm boy in Miguel's class who has
muscles where the rest of the boys can only imagine them. "My name means 'death' in French,"
he likes to brag, pounding his chest as if he were
Tarzan. His family came to Vermont from
Canada in the nineteenth century, before the
skiers and vacationers and college students arrived. He likes to brag about that, too. But Mort
doesn't get very good grades, and some of the

town boys make fun of his homemade haircut and clothes from the Second Hand.

"Meatballs! Yum, my favorite." Mort pops one of Tía Lola's treats into his mouth.

Miguel expects Mort to spit it up or keel over dead. Instead, Mort helps himself to another. "Don't mind if I do!" He laughs. "Hey, these are delicious!"

That afternoon, it might be a coincidence, but it certainly is a first: Mort spells Mississippi correctly during the spelling bee.

There is one treat left in Miguel's lunchbox. On the way to baseball practice, he pops it into his mouth.

Miguel thinks of asking his mom about the strange treat, but it is Tía Lola who always fixes their lunches. "Tía Lola," he begins, showing her the crumpled-up tinfoil. But before he can ask about the magic treat, Tía Lola is hugging and kissing him. She is so pleased he likes her *quipes*. They are made of grain and ground meat and a dash of pepper, and they will put muscles on his arms.

Miguel doesn't care what they are called. Are

they magic? "I have to make the team, Tía Lola,"
he adds.

Tía Lola nods. *"Yo sé."*

Of course she knows! She is a *santera*, Miguel
reminds himself. She works magic.

At lunch the next day, Miguel finds a half-
dozen chewy fritters in a plastic container. Mort
has four and Miguel two. Tía Lola says the chewy
treats are called *empanaditas de queso*, and they
are made of cheese and dough fried in peanut oil.

The following morning, Mort reports a piece
of luck to Miguel. His pop just found out he'd won
five hundred dollars on his weekly lottery ticket!
Since Mort helped pick out the winning number,
his father is going to buy him his very own heifer
to show at the county fair that August.

"Awesome," Miguel says, trying to make his
voice sound as if he thinks that is an exciting
purchase. Meanwhile, his own lucky surprise arrives in the mail. A Sammy Sosa Louisville Slug-
ger his father has sent up from New York for good
luck in the upcoming tryouts.

Every day when he wakes up, Miguel takes imaginary swings at an imaginary ball with his new

bat. He flexes his arms, but the muscles are still pretty soft. Still, he definitely feels stronger. Tía Lola's special magic rations in his lunchbox are working.

He asks her about the jars she brought from the island. She explains that they are potions made from *hierbabuena* and *guayuyo* and *yema de huevos* to put on sores and cuts.

"Magic potions?" he wants to know.

She smiles and pushes the hair back from his eyes. "*Todo es mágico si se hace con amor, Miguel.*"

That is too corny for words—in English or Spanish. Everything is magic if made with love? Oh, please, and *por favor!*

But, of course, it is just like a *santera* to be secretive, Miguel thinks. He winks back, pretending to go along with Tía Lola. After all, in this country, she can probably be arrested for working magic so her nephew can make the local baseball team.

That night on the phone, Miguel confesses to his father that Tía Lola is putting magic foods in his lunchbox to help him make the team.

"It means a lot to you to make that team, doesn't it, *tiguerito?*" his father observes.

It does mean a lot. After all, his only two friends are already on the team. "Ah, Miguel, come on, you're a shoo-in," Sam keeps saying to him.

Dean agrees. "Yeah, you're Dominican. I mean, baseball's, like, natural for you."

When Miguel tells his father what Dean has said, his father gets annoyed. "You'll make the team because you've been practicing hard, that's why." Papi often says that the worst thing you can do to people is make assumptions about them. Stereotyping, he calls it.

Perhaps he, Miguel, is making assumptions about Tía Lola. Maybe she isn't working magic on him. After all, she tells him the name of everything she cooks and exactly what she puts in it. Besides, she also fixes the same things in Juanita's lunchbox, and Miguel hasn't noticed any improvements in the little-sister department.

What Miguel doesn't tell his father is that Tía Lola isn't the only one who is trying to work a little magic. Often, when he is driving to town with Mami to get groceries or do some Saturday errand, Miguel will think to himself: *If the traffic light changes to green before we reach the corner, I'll make the team.*

Sometimes just before they reach the corner, the light changes to green. Miguel feels a rush of relief and joy. But just as many times, the light is still red. Miguel sits in the front seat beside his mother, scowling, and thinking, *I mean, the very next light, not this one.*

He worries that he is letting himself get too jumpy and superstitious. But he keeps hoping his wishes will come true:

If the phone rings in the next minute, I'll get an A on my math exam.

If we pass seven red cars before we get home, I'll make a lot of new friends.

If I see a falling star...a double rainbow...a unicorn...a space alien—

This wish requires higher and higher stakes—

My parents will get back together again.

The weekend of the tryouts a most magical thing does happen. His father comes up from New York to give Miguel "moral support."

"Kind of like Tía Lola's magic," his father explains.

Saturday morning, they all drive over to the school playground—Papi and Mami and Juanita and Tía Lola, just like a real family. The field is already full of players who made the team last year. Miguel spots Dean in the outfield and Sam manning first base. Rudy, in gray sweatpants and sporting a Red Sox cap, is calling instructions to the rookies who have come to try out.

Miguel joins the lineup of boys waiting to bat. Suddenly, he wishes stereotypes were true, and he could automatically make the team *because* his parents come from the Dominican Republic.

He glances over at the bleachers, where his family is sitting, and one of his superstitious wishing-thoughts pops into his head. *If Tía Lola gives me a sign, I'll make the team.*

He closes his eyes tight, shutting out such silly thoughts. This is no time to spook himself with superstitions. *Miguel Guzmán,* he tells himself, *you're going to make this team because you've practiced hard and you deserve to win!*

At that moment, just as he opens his eyes, Tía Lola waves her yellow scarf.

He swings and the ball goes flying up, high and far, all the power of her Dominican cooking behind it and all the magic of her love behind that.

Chapter Five

▼▼▼

The Spanish Word War

Their father is having a private talk with their mother in the kitchen. Now that the weather is nice, he drives up every other weekend to see Miguel and Juanita. Once school is out, he wants them to come down and visit him in the city. But their mother is obviously not in agreement. Voices are rising in the kitchen.

Juanita hurries to her brother's side. Miguel can tell she is about to cry. He is not going to get upset. When things get bad, he just daydreams about baseball.

But now his sister's tearful face is getting between him and a fly ball.

In order to catch it, he pushes her aside. She stumbles, falls, then bursts into tears and runs upstairs.

Miguel crouches, catches the imaginary ball,

and throws it to the catcher. The crowd stands and roars. His buddies on the team slap him on the back.

But somehow he doesn't feel as good as he thought he would.

He knocks on his sister's door.

"*Se puede.*" Tía Lola calls out permission for him to enter.

Their aunt is sitting on the bed with a tearful Juanita. "*Tienes que cuidar a tu hermanita,*" Tía Lola begins when she sees her nephew.

"I know I have to take care of *mi hermanita,* Tía Lola," Miguel agrees. He speaks to his aunt in Spanglish. Spanglish is what his mother and father call the English with a sprinkling of Spanish that Miguel and Juanita speak when they think they are speaking Spanish. "It's just *que* sometimes Juanita *es una* baby—"

"I am *not* a baby!" Juanita howls.

Tía Lola puts an arm around each one. "*¡Ya, ya!*" she pretends to scold them. They are brother and sister. They must not fight. They need to do something together so they will learn to get along.

"Maybe she can learn to throw a baseball?"

Miguel suggests. He smirks at his sister, who sticks her tongue out at him.

Tía Lola's face suddenly lights up. She has a great idea: her niece and her nephew can give her English classes together!

Miguel's face falls. He doesn't want to spend the upcoming summer doing anything that resembles schoolwork. "But you don't want to speak English," Miguel reminds her.

"English is too hard, Tía Lola, really," Juanita adds.

For the first time all day, brother and sister agree on something.

Already, Tía Lola's idea is working.

Miguel definitely owes his aunt a favor or two. He is still convinced that back in early spring, she worked some magic to help him make the team. But why does his aunt suddenly want to learn English after months of refusing to do so? "*¿Por qué, Tía Lola?*"

Their aunt looks rather shy, which is hard for Tía Lola to do with her lively face and bright eyes. She has an admission to make. Their mother has asked her to turn her visit into a stay. She can be of more help to everyone if she knows more English. And to repay her niece and nephew for teaching her English, Tía Lola is going to teach them more Spanish.

"*Yo sé mucho español*," Miguel protests. He knows a lot of Spanish.

"I know more Spanish than you." Juanita smirks.

It is Miguel's turn to stick his tongue out at her.

While Mami and Papi continue their discussion in the kitchen, Miguel begins the first lesson. "Tía Lola, we're going to learn names." He speaks slowly as if he were talking to an old person with a hearing problem. "What is your name?"

Tía Lola repeats, "What is your name?"

"No, no." Juanita shakes her head. "You have to say, 'My name is Lola.'"

"No, no," Tía Lola says, pronouncing every word carefully. "You have to say—"

"It's no use," Miguel tells his sister. "She doesn't really understand what she is saying."

"She doesn't really understand what she is saying," Tía Lola rattles on.

Their mother comes to the door, their father behind her. "What's going on here?" she asks.

Miguel cannot tell from looking at their faces what agreement they have come to.

"We're teaching Tía Lola English," Miguel explains. And then, remembering that one of the main reasons their mother has given for not letting them visit their father is that they are too young to travel alone, he adds, "Maybe Tía Lola can go down to New York with us if she knows a little English."

"She can take care of us," Juanita adds.

"We'll see," their mother says. It is what she always says when she hasn't made up her mind whether to say yes or no to something they ask her for.

Every opportunity they have, Miguel and Juanita give their aunt an English lesson.

On the walk to town, Miguel stops at the sign beside the covered bridge. "Load limit: one ton."

"Load-limit-one-ton," Tía Lola repeats.

In town, Miguel points to the signs with the names of the streets they are waiting to cross. Hardscrabble, Main, College, and his favorite, Painter, because it reminds him of his father. Then the traffic signs. "One way," he calls off. "Caution."

The crossing guard holds up her stop sign to the traffic. "Have a nice day," she says when they have crossed safely to the other side.

"One-way-caution-you're-welcome-thanks-for-asking," Tía Lola chatters on. That is the problem with Tía Lola's English. Whenever she begins speaking it, she speaks all of it, all together.

The crossing guard looks worried. "Have-a-nice-day," Tía Lola concludes. Sometimes, by chance, she says just the right phrase.

Down the street, walking toward them, comes Mrs. Prouty, accompanied by her chubby twin daughters. Miguel tries to steer Tía Lola into Scents and Spirits, Stargazer's candle and card shop, but Mrs. Prouty has caught sight of them. "How nice to see you, Miguel. This must be the aunt your mother was telling me about."

Miguel is so flustered, he mixes up everybody's name. Mrs. Prouty's daughters giggle and reach out to shake Tía Lola's hand. But that is not Tía Lola's way to greet a person.

"Load-limit-one-ton," Tía Lola coos, hugging the girls, whose round faces turn pink. "Slippery-when-wet-proceed-with-caution." Mrs. Prouty looks perplexed. Especially when Tía Lola throws her arms around her, too.

"Awesome-get-a-life-chill-out," Tía Lola chants. Miguel cringes. He has been teaching Tía Lola some slang expressions in order to make her sound a little more cool in English.

"It is a bit chilly for June, isn't it?" Mrs. Prouty is saying, her jaw even stiffer than usual as she ushers her girls past the demented woman.

Miguel is eager to get Tía Lola home before she embarrasses them any further.

As they are walking past the post office, their mailman comes down the steps.

"Where-is-the-ladies'-room?" Tía Lola greets him.

The young man scratches his head and hurries away.

"*Mi inglés no funciona,*" Tía Lola finally admits. Her English isn't working. She makes friends easier when she just speaks Spanish to everyone. Her magic doesn't seem to work in a second language.

"You have to practice, Tía Lola," Miguel reminds her. "You have to know what to say when."

But every day Tía Lola cannot wait for her English lesson to be over. Then it is Miguel's and Juanita's turn to try to get along in their second language, Spanish.

* * *

Actually, Miguel and Juanita are not getting along any better in Spanish than in English. They are fighting more now that they have two languages to do it in. The fights get worse when they learn from their aunt that in Spanish, words have gender.

"What does *that* mean?" Juanita wants to know. Are some words pretty and feminine and some—she looks over at her brother—ugly and mean?

Tía Lola tries to explain. In Spanish, words have to be masculine or feminine. She doesn't know exactly why that is. The male words usually end in *o*, and the female words in *a*. Like the word for sky, *cielo*, is masculine, while the word for earth, *tierra*, is feminine.

"We get the sky! We get the sky!" Miguel can't help gloating at his sister. It's as if they are playing Monopoly and he has just bought Boardwalk.

"Well, we own the earth! It ends in *a*. *La tierra!*" It is Juanita's turn to gloat. "And everything in the sky: *la luna, la lluvia, las estrellas!*"

Tía Lola is shaking her head. That's not the way it works. Boys don't own the sky. Girls don't own the earth, the moon, the rain, and the stars. But neither Miguel nor Juanita is listening anymore.

Summer is here! On the way home from the last day of class, Miguel thinks of all the things he has to look forward to. Team practice will soon start up. Hopefully, he will get to visit his father and friends in New York. Meanwhile, Tía Lola is full of ideas for fun things for Miguel and Juanita to do.

The first day of vacation, they begin planting a garden in the backyard. Tía Lola slips on her highest of heels as if she were going out to a nightclub instead of to the backyard. Then, as she walks and zigzags and swerves up and down, making rows, Juanita and Miguel follow behind her, dropping seeds in the holes she makes with her heels.

They plant lettuce and *verduras, tomaticos,* and black beans from packets Tía Lola brought from the island. They clean the raspberry canes, which are already studded with bright crimson fruit. "I love these," Miguel says, picking mouthfuls as he works away.

Unfortunately, the blue jays and redwing blackbirds love them, too. But Tía Lola thinks of a solution. She brings out all her mantillas and drapes them over the raspberry bushes. Now when the birds swoop down, all they get is a few threads in their beaks. Miguel even feels a little sorry for them. He puts out a handful of berries in a dish so the birds can have a treat, too.

Soon green shoots are coming out of the ground in fanciful, zigzaggy rows. It turns out Tía Lola has laid out the garden in the shape of the island! Where her hometown would be on the map, she has planted *berenjenas,* her favorite vegetable, eggplants. For the border between the Dominican Republic and its neighbor, Haiti, she orders a special kind of rosebush without thorns. "For a rosier future between the two countries," she explains in Spanish. She reserves her hot chili peppers for the spot where the capital would be. *"Para los políticos por las mentiras que dicen."* Miguel does not understand. For the politicians because of the lies they tell? Tía Lola laughs. It is a kind of adult joke you have to keep up with the news to understand.

At the center of the garden, Tía Lola posts her beloved Dominican flag. Then she puts her hand on her heart and sings the national anthem, which she is trying to teach her niece and nephew to sing. It is the first time Miguel has seen his aunt teary-eyed. Mami explains that Tía Lola is understandably homesick from time to time. Having these reminders and rituals from home makes her feel a little less far away from her country and the rest of the family.

Of course, the raccoons don't care a hoot about Tía Lola's map. They start eating up the little shoots of lettuce and eggplant and shred the rosebushes to bits. But Tía Lola figures out a way to outsmart them as well. She ties her maracas to a pair of broomsticks and sticks the broomsticks in the ground by the garden. All day and all night, as the breeze blows on them, they clackety-clack, scaring away the raccoons.

But the most fun for Miguel is when they go out with garden shears and prune the bushes in the shapes of parrots and palm trees, monkeys and huge butterflies. Everyone who drives by stops to marvel at the transformed property.

"Keep-out-no-trespassing," Tía Lola greets them, and quickly they get back in their cars and drive away.

* * *

If Miguel thinks Tía Lola is having a hard time catching on to plain English, using expressions around her proves downright dangerous.

"Becky has a green thumb," Mami remarks one day as she comes in the door with a bunch of basil their neighbor has given her.

"*¡Emergencia!*" Tía Lola cries out. The thumb could be gangrenous! She reaches for the phone. Mami has taught her to dial 911 if there is ever an emergency.

"*¡No, no, Tía Lola!*" Mami stops her. The phrase is an expression in English that means that Becky is good with plants.

Then why didn't she say so? Tía Lola asks, very reasonably for once.

The afternoon of the first big thunderstorm, Juanita and Miguel are playing outside. They come running in the house, soaking wet. "It's raining cats and dogs!" Miguel remarks as he throws off his jacket.

"*¡No me diga!*" Tía Lola says, running out with a broom to chase the stray cats and dogs away from the front lawn. She slips on the wet steps and goes tumbling down, head over heels. Thank goodness only the broom snaps in two, though the next morning Tía Lola's whole right side is black and blue.

* * *

Their mother has still not made up her mind about letting Miguel and his sister visit their father in New York.

"Mami, please, before practice starts up," Miguel pleads. In a few weeks, the team will have daily practice, and Miguel does not want to miss one day of it.

But his mother is not convinced. Tía Lola is still lost in English. Traveling with her would be traveling with an adult who couldn't really take care of them if they ran into a problem. Furthermore, the way that Miguel and Juanita are always arguing, they cannot be trusted to go anywhere together.

"I promise I'll try," Miguel offers. He'll do anything in order to visit his father and friends and see New York City again. Even if it involves getting along with his little sister.

"I have to see some improvement first," his mother declares.

Miguel finds his sister in her bedroom. She is putting her dolls in the cradles their father has made for her. They are cut out of cardboard and colored with bright designs. Every time Papi drives up to visit, he brings a new one along.

"Truce, Nita!" Miguel holds up his hands. "I mean it. You can have *cielo, dinero, carro*—all the *o* words you want."

Juanita glances up. A look of suspicion spreads across her face. She can have *sky, money, car?*

Miguel nods, but he can see she is not quite sure what to make of her brother's sudden generosity. He decides to tell his sister the truth. "Mami's not going to let us go to New York unless she sees us getting along." And there is one other thing. "We've got to get Tía Lola to say just a few things right so Mami feels okay about her English."

"How are we going to do that?" Juanita abandons her dolls to work out a plan with her brother. They are quiet a moment, thinking. "I know, I know," she pipes up. "It'll be like the crossing lady. We'll draw some signs on some cards and flash them to Tía Lola when Mami is around."

"Great idea!" Miguel says, before he remembers it is his dumb little sister who has come up with it.

* * *

They draw a plate beside a red stop sign. They explain to their aunt that when they flash her that card, she should say, "I can't eat another bite" in English.

"I-can't-eat-another-bite," Tía Lola practices.

"*Muy bien, Tía Lola,*" Miguel says. Very good.

On another card, Juanita draws a round bowl that looks sort of like a toilet bowl. She colors it pink. When Tía Lola sees that card, she has to say, "Where is the ladies' room?"

On still another card, they draw a bright sun with a smiley face. "Have a nice day!" Miguel rehearses for his aunt.

"Have-a-nice-day!" Tía Lola repeats, smiling at the smiley face. "Where-is-the-ladies'-room-I-can't-eat-another-bite."

"*No, Tía Lola,*" Juanita explains. "*Una a la vez.*" Just say one at a time. Juanita holds up one finger while Miguel flashes one card. They practice several times.

Finally, Tía Lola understands what they want. It is gratifying when that happens. Their mother always says that the easiest language to learn but the hardest to speak is *mutual understanding*. It is easy because you don't even have to speak it with words, but hard because you never can seem to find the right person to speak it to.

At Rudy's Restaurant for brunch that Sunday, their mother praises Miguel and Juanita for getting along so well lately. "I'm really proud of you guys for making an effort."

It's just a plot so you'll let us go to New York, Miguel feels like saying. But it's not so bad to be getting along with his little sister.

Across the table, Tía Lola is hungrily eating forkfuls of Rudy's sourdough pancakes. It is time for step two of the plan.

Miguel reaches into his pocket. He is sitting next to his mother so she cannot see his left hand. He holds up the card with the drawing of a plate and stop sign and coughs.

Tía Lola looks up and smiles at the card. "I can't eat another bite," she says in perfect English. But she keeps right on shoveling pancake into her mouth.

Quickly, Miguel pulls Tía Lola's plate toward him and offers to finish it. Before Tía Lola can protest, he holds up the drawing of the pink bowl.

"Where is the ladies' room?" Tía Lola asks out loud. The waitress, happening by, says, "Just follow me."

But Tía Lola remains sitting.

"Come on, Tía Lola," Juanita urges, taking her aunt by the hand. "I've got to go, too." Tía Lola looks a bit unsure, but she is game for whatever is going on.

Miguel's mother watches as Tía Lola and Juanita walk toward the back of the restaurant. "Tía Lola's English sure has improved," she notes thoughtfully.

Now is the moment to pop the question. Miguel takes a deep breath. "So, Mami, can we go to New York?"

Miguel can see the conflicting emotions on his mother's face. She will miss them if they leave, but she knows that it is important to let them go. She looks at him for a long moment, and then her face relaxes. He understands that means yes.

"You'll take good care of them, won't you, Miguel?" his mother asks, nodding toward Tía Lola and Juanita, who are returning from the bathroom.

"Of course I will, Mami," Miguel promises.

As his sister sits down, Miguel looks straight at her and smiles. She smiles back. They are speaking the language of mutual understanding without having to say a single word! *We're going to New York,* his look says.

I can't wait! her smile replies.

Rudy comes out from the kitchen to say hello. He has been swamped with the brunch crowd, and he finally has a minute. He ruffles Miguel's hair and asks Tía Lola how she likes his pancakes. "By the way, can I get you folks a piece of my summertime specialty, mud pie, compliments of the house?"

"I can't eat another bite," Mami says as she bends over and picks up a couple of cards that have fallen on the floor. "I think these are yours," she says, winking at Miguel. She lays the cards on the table: a red stop sign and a pink bowl. "By the way," she asks Juanita, as if she doesn't already know, "where *is* the ladies' room?"

Chapter Six

▼▼▼

Three Happy Days in *Nueva* York

Finally, in late June, Miguel and Juanita travel down to New York City to visit their father. They take a train, accompanied by Tía Lola. When they arrive at Pennsylvania Station, their father is waiting for them. They hug and laugh and tell him all about their exciting trip past yellow-ocher hay bales, cadmium-red barns, raw-umber cows, and the Hudson River. When the excitement dies down, their father looks around. "Where did Tía Lola go?"

"Where did Tía Lola go?" Juanita repeats, as if she were Tía Lola having her English lesson.

"Yes, where did Tía Lola go? She was standing right here with us." And there is her suitcase, but no Tía Lola! Their father looks worried. If their mother finds out, she will say it is just like their father to lose their aunt in New York City.

Maybe she won't let Miguel and Juanita come back for a second visit.

"Tía Lola!" they shout, but the din of the crowd drowns out their voices.

"Let's not get upset," their father says, his voice rising, sounding very upset. "She's got my address, right?"

"I'm not sure," Miguel replies, reaching into his pocket and pulling out the slip of paper on which his mother has written down their father's address and phone number. "But I think she doesn't."

They walk around and look for her in all the shops. Miguel even tries paging his aunt as he did the day she arrived at the Burlington Airport. But Tía Lola doesn't show up at the information booth. She is *really* lost this time.

When Tía Lola doesn't come back for an hour, they decide it's time to do more than just look for her themselves. They fill out a report at the police office at Penn Station. Then they head to their father's apartment to wait for the police to call them. As they are opening the door of their father's loft, the phone rings.

"Oh, hi there, Linda, how you doin'?" their father says, trying to hide the worry in his voice. He puts his hand over the receiver and mouths, *Your mother.* As he listens, his eyes close in pain. "I'm really sorry about this. The kids and I—" His father pulls the phone away from his ear as if he doesn't like what he is hearing. "I'll get off now so the line can be free when she calls."

"Tía Lola called your mother in Vermont," he explains when he gets off the phone. "I guess she knew that number by heart." Miguel and Juanita nod. "Your mother gave her my number. She's going to call here. We can ask her to read off the street signs and we can go get her." He is trying to sound cheerful. "Your mother's pretty upset."

Miguel feels bad. After all, he promised his mother that he would take care of his little sister and aunt. "It wasn't your fault, Papi."

"Tell that to your mother," their father sighs.

"We will," Miguel and Juanita say, almost at the same time. But Miguel wonders if it will really help, or just get them all in bigger trouble.

The phone rings.

"Tía Lola!" their father shouts into the

phone. *"No te preocupes."* She is not to worry.
They will come and get her. All she has to do is
step out of the booth and read the names of the
streets. There should be two signs on the corner.
His face looks relieved. The worry lines on his
forehead have disappeared.

But in a minute, the worry lines are back.
"No, no, no, Tía Lola." Papi puts his hand over
the receiver. "She tells me she's at the corner of
Stop and One Way!"

Miguel reaches for the phone. "Maybe I can
explain it better. I've been teaching her street
signs in Vermont."

"Hola, Tía Lola," Miguel begins. Very calmly,
he explains that the signs she has reported tell
drivers how to drive. Does she remember how in
Vermont they also practiced reading the names
of streets at each corner?

Before Tía Lola can answer, a mechanical
voice comes on, saying to put another dime in
the machine or the call will be disconnected.
Miguel can hear the coins dropping inside the
machine. Tía Lola has understood without his
translation! *"Yo comprendo,"* his aunt is saying.
"Un momento, Miguel."

Miguel waits and his father waits and Juanita

waits and their mother in Vermont waits to hear that their aunt has been found. And then Tía Lola is back on the line with the names of the streets. *"Estoy en la treinta y cuatro y quinta."* She is on Thirty-fourth and Fifth. She is looking up at a very, very, very tall building whose top floor must be at heaven's front door!

"Just stay right there, Tía Lola," Miguel tells her. "We'll come and get you."

When they arrive at the Empire State Building, Tía Lola is standing beside a phone booth, waving. Miguel and Juanita run down the street toward her.

"Mi culpa," Tía Lola says. It is all her fault. She has never seen such sights. She started to walk and look around, and soon she was lost.

"What do you say we get something to eat?" Miguel's father asks cheerfully.

"There's something I have to do first," Miguel says. He enters the phone booth and picks up the receiver. When his mother answers in Vermont, Miguel speaks in Spanish because he knows that will make her feel happy. *"Hola, Mami. Encontramos a Tía Lola. No te preocupes."* We found Tía Lola. Don't worry.

And then, very quietly, so no one can over-hear him, he whispers, *"Te quiero mucho."*

"What do you want to do today?" their father asks them the next morning. They have all slept very well after the excitement of the previous evening.

"I want to see my friends and go to a Yankees game," Miguel pipes up. "José says they're play-ing today."

"I want to go to the zoo," Juanita disagrees. "I want to see the penguins."

"The zoo is kid stuff," Miguel tells his sister.

"I *am* a kid!" Juanita states. "And you're a kid, too."

"Am not!" Miguel stands up to his full height.

Their father is sitting on a stool beside one of his paintings. He rolls his eyes and sighs. "I had forgotten," he announces to no one in particular, "the happy pitter-patter of little feet...."

From behind the screen that separates her guest "room" from the rest of the loft, Tía Lola emerges. Her *moño* is lopsided on top of her head and she is rubbing her eyes. *"Buenos días,"* she says, looking from one to the other. She heard raised voices. What is going on? Are the kids arguing again?

"Miguel says he is not a kid," Juanita reports.

"Miguel es un hombrecito," Tía Lola agrees with her nephew. He is a little man. Look how he saved the day yesterday.

"Juanita wants to go to a stupid zoo," Miguel says, feeling encouraged. "Wouldn't you rather go to a ball game than to the zoo, Tía Lola?"

"Let's go to the zoo, Tía Lola," Juanita pleads. "Please!"

Tía Lola considers a moment. Since they have three days in New York, why not have each person choose a day to do a favorite thing. *"¿Qué te parece, Daniel?"*

Their father thinks this is a super idea. "We'll start with Miguel's choice because I believe there is a Yankees game today; then tomorrow we can spend the day at the zoo for Juanita's turn. Tía Lola can choose something for the last day before you take the train back in the late afternoon."

"¿Y tú?" Tía Lola asks their father. What about his turn?

"I'm getting my wish by having you all here with me," he explains. "But one thing, guys. Your grandparents really want to see you."

"What are you going to choose for your turn, Tía Lola?" Juanita wants to know.

Tía Lola shakes her head. She doesn't need a turn. No matter what they do, she is going to have fun. She smiles at Juanita. She winks at Miguel.

Sometimes you can't really tell whose side Tía Lola is on.

The afternoon clouds up. By the time they set out, it is raining lightly. "*¡Sin gatos, sin perros!*" Tía Lola says, laughing. Without cats or dogs! Tía Lola is really catching on to English.

They take the subway out to Yankee Stadium, where they meet up with Miguel's friend José and his big brother, Leonel. Even with the rain, the crowd stretches out to the parking lot. When they finally get their tickets, their seats are way up high in the grandstand. They might as well be on a small plane staring down at the diamond.

But when the Yankees run out to play ball,

Miguel and José stand up on their seats, fingers at their lips, and whistle. Every time a pinstriped blob comes up to bat, Tía Lola hugs the boys, spilling the popcorn they have bought, until there is hardly any left in the bucket. Everyone seems to be having a great time. Even Juanita. She jumps up and down hollering whenever the Yankees get a hit. She has decided she really loves baseball after all.

On the way back to Papi's place, they stop for pizza. Miguel has to admit that it is not as good as Tía Lola's pizza, but he doesn't care. He is sitting opposite one of his best friends in the world and the Yankees have won.

When they get home that night, the phone is ringing. "Why don't you get that?" Miguel's father says, nodding. "It's probably your mother. She'll want to know what trouble I've gotten you into today."

Miguel answers the phone. His father is a mind reader. "*Hola, Mami,*" he says brightly. "We went to a Yankees game. José came, too. It was real exciting." But then, just because her voice sounds lonely on the other end, he adds, "The popcorn was stale. No, no, that's not *all* we had for dinner. Juanita got laryngitis from screaming so much. It rained."

* * *

That evening, before going to bed, their father unveils his latest painting.

The background is painted a pale gray, but you almost can't see the gray, because of all the bursts of red and gold and purple strokes, like fireworks on the Fourth of July. Miguel is sure his father will start quizzing them on the names of the colors.

But instead, Papi asks, "So what d'you think?"

"What is it?" Miguel wants to know.

"Use your imagination. Right, Papi?" Juanita says.

"I mean, what's it called?" Miguel says, narrowing his eyes at his sister.

"Actually, *tiguerito*, it's called *Untitled*," their father says, smiling. "But maybe you or Juanita would like to title it. Why don't we have a contest, eh? For the next day or so, think about what we might name it."

"What does the winner get?" Miguel asks.

"Let's see," their father considers. "An all-expenses-paid trip to New York with a brother or sister of your choice."

"If I win, can I substitute a friend?" Miguel asks.

* * *

The next day is sunshiny and warm. The perfect day for going to the zoo. Juanita gets to invite Ming, her special friend from first grade, to come along, too.

They visit the penguins, Juanita pointing excitedly at some baby ones who are learning to waddle single file behind their mother and father. Miguel has to admit it is kind of fun to watch them in their little tuxedo suits, looking like waiters in a fancy restaurant. "I'll have a well-done cheeseburger and fries and a Coke," he says, tapping at the glass wall. Ming thinks Miguel's remark is so funny, she repeats it at the snake house.

After lunch, they visit the dolphins, Miguel's favorite animal. He hangs over the rail and watches a dolphin leap through a hoop the trainer holds up. Someday, when he gets tired of being a major league baseball player, Miguel is going to be a trainer of dolphins.

When the dolphin show is over, Miguel says, "Let's go see the tigers, my other favorite animal." After all, his father's nickname for him is *tiguerito*, which means "little tiger."

"Hey, what d'you say your sister gets to pick? Remember, this is her day."

"It's okay, Papi," Juanita says. "The zoo is kid stuff. Let Miguel enjoy himself."

"The zoo is kid stuff!" Ming repeats, giggling, as the two girls link hands and skip all the way to the tigers.

The next morning, they hop on a subway to see Abuelito and Abuelita. Papi and his parents came to the United States when Papi was only seven years old, Juanita's age. For twenty-nine years, his parents have lived in Brooklyn, where they still own a bodega filled with lots of things from the Dominican Republic.

The minute they step out of the subway station, Tía Lola's ears perk up. Everyone is speaking Spanish! The *moño* on top of her head stands taller. Her lipstick shines redder. The beauty mark above her upper lip winks like a star. It is as if she were back home on the island.

They walk for blocks without hearing a word of English. Most of the shops have spilled outdoors into the streets. Colorful dresses hang from racks on the sidewalks, and bins overflow with tropical fruits and vegetables, which they have not seen for months in the Grand Union in Vermont.

"*Aguacates*, avocados. *Plátanos*, plantains. *Auyama*, squash. *Piña*, pineapple. *Batata*, sweet potato," Tía Lola calls out, matching up her Spanish with her English.

Meanwhile, Papi is pointing left and right. "Viridian," Miguel guesses, "olive green, crimson, dioxazine purple." This last color is one Papi has just taught them. To Miguel, dioxazine sounds more like the name of a medicine than of a deep, rich purple.

Up ahead, Abuelito and Abuelita are sitting in chairs on the sidewalk in front of their bodega. Miguel and Juanita race down the street toward them.

They kiss and hug, and then, as if they've forgotten that they had already done so, they kiss and hug again. "Tell us all about Vermont," Abuelita says. And for the next half hour, that's exactly what Miguel and Juanita do.

Finally, their Papi reminds them, "Remember, kids, it's Tía Lola's day. She gets to choose what we do now. *Bueno*, Tía Lola, now you *do* have to tell us what you want. Tía Lola? Where did your Tía Lola go?" Miguel's father is turning around in circles.

He has a worried look on his face. It will be terrible if they lose Tía Lola a second time in three days!

But, no, there she is, down the street, under a sign that reads SOUNDS OF QUISQUEYA and LAVANDERÍA TROPICAL. Tía Lola is dancing the merengue with one of the shopkeepers right on the sidewalk. Other people are joining in.

"I think this is exactly what Tía Lola wants to be doing on her last day in New York," their father remarks.

Late that afternoon, they stop to get their bags at Papi's loft on the way to the train station. His new painting, still untitled, is propped up on an easel.

"Oops, we forgot the contest!" their father says. "What are we going to name it?"

It doesn't take long for Tía Lola to speak up. The Yankees, José, Ming, the penguins, merengue on the sidewalk, the colors, the fun: she points here and there in the painting. "*Tres días alegres en Nueva York,*" she suggests. And then to show off how much English she has learned on this trip, she translates, "*Three Happy Days in* Nueva York."

"Your turn, Miguel and Juanita," their father says.

But neither one can think of a better name for the painting or a better way to describe their visit.

"It's settled," their papi says, removing the canvas from its frame and rolling it up. "Tía Lola, you have just won an all-expenses-paid second trip to New York with your niece and nephew. And an original painting by the artist Daniel Guzmán."

"I think it's better if I keep the painting here," Tía Lola says, looking at the children for help. She doesn't want to hurt their father's feelings. But their mother will certainly not appreciate *Three Happy Days in* Nueva *York* hanging in their farmhouse in Vermont.

"I think it's a good idea to keep it here," Miguel says.

"Yes, Papi," Juanita agrees. "Then we can visit it, too, when we come again soon."

So the painting stays in New York. But Miguel and Juanita and their aunt carry the memories of those three happy days with them back to Vermont.

Chapter Seven

▼▼▼

Two Happy Months in Vermont

The long, sweet, sunny days of summer come one after another after another. Each one is like a piece of fancy candy in a gold-and-blue wrapper.

Most nights, now that school is out, Tía Lola tells stories, sometimes until very late. The uncle who fell in love with a *ciguapa* and never married. The beautiful cousin who never cut her hair and carried it around in a wheelbarrow. The grandfather whose eyes turned blue when he saw his first grandchild.

Some nights, for a break, they explore the old house. In the attic, behind their own boxes, they find dusty trunks full of yellowing letters and photographs. Miguel discovers several faded photos of a group of boys all lined up in old-fashioned baseball uniforms. Except for the funny caps and knickers and knee socks, the boys in the photos could be any of the boys on Miguel's team. One photo of a boy with a baseball glove in his hand is inscribed, *Charlebois, '34.*

Miguel tries to imagine the grouchy old man at Rudy's Restaurant as the young boy with the friendly smile in the photograph.

But he can't see even a faint resemblance.

Since the team doesn't have a good place for daily practice, Miguel's mother suggests they use the back pasture behind the house. "But let me write Colonel Charlebois first, just in case."

Their landlord lives in a big white house in the center of town. He has already written them once this summer, complaining about "the unseemly shape of the vegetation," after Tía Lola trimmed the hedges in front of the house in the shapes of pineapples and parrots and palm trees.

"Can't you just call him and ask him, Mami?" Miguel asks. After all, the team is impatient to get started with practice. A letter will take several days to be answered.

"You try calling him," Miguel's mother says, holding out the phone. Miguel dials the number his mother reads from a card tacked on the kitchen bulletin board. The phone rings once, twice. A machine clicks on, and a cranky old voice speaks up: "This is Colonel Charles Charlebois. I can't be bothered coming to the phone every time it rings. If you have a message, you can write me at 27 Main Street, Middlebury, Vermont 05753."

"Let's write that letter, shall we?" Mami says, taking the phone back from Miguel.

Two days later, Colonel Charlebois's answer is in their mailbox. It has not been postmarked. He must have driven out and delivered it himself.

"I would be honored to have the team practice in my back pasture," he replies in a shaky hand as if he'd written the letter while riding in a car over a bumpy road.

"Honored!" Miguel's mother says, lifting her eyebrows. She translates the letter for Tía Lola, who merely nods as if she'd known all along that Colonel Charlebois is really a nice man.

And so every day Miguel's friends come over, and the team plays ball in the back field where only six months ago, Miguel (or maybe it was the *ciguapas*?) wrote a great big welcome to Tía

Lola. Twice a week, Rudy drops by to coach. They play all afternoon, and afterward when they are hot and sweaty, Tía Lola invites them inside for cool, refreshing smoothies, which she calls *frío-fríos*. As they slurp and lick, she practices her English by telling them wonderful stories about Dominican baseball players like Sammy Sosa and the Alou brothers and Juan Marichal and Pedro and Ramón Martínez. The way she tells the stories, it's as if she knows these players personally. Miguel and his friends are enthralled.

After a couple of weeks of practice, the team votes to make Miguel the captain. José, who is visiting from New York, substitutes for whoever is missing that day. Tía Lola is named manager.

"*¿Y qué hace el manager?*" Tía Lola wants to know what a manager does.

"A manager makes us *frío-fríos*," Captain Miguel says.

Every day, after practice, there are *frío-fríos* in a tall pitcher in the icebox.

It is a happy summer—

Until Tía Lola decides to paint the house purple.

* * *

Miguel and his friends have been playing ball in the back field—their view of the house shielded by the maple trees. As they walk back from practice, they look up.

"Holy cow!" Miguel cries out.

The front porch is the color of a bright bruise. Miguel can't help thinking of the deep, rich purple whose name he recently learned from his father in New York. "Dioxazine," he mutters to himself. The rest of the house is still the same color as almost every other house in town. "Regulation white," Papi calls it whenever he comes up to visit and drives through town.

In her high heels and a dress with flowers whose petals match the color of the porch stands Tía Lola, painting broad purple strokes.

For a brief second, Miguel feels a flash of that old embarrassment he used to feel about his crazy aunt.

"Awesome," his friend Dean is saying.

"Cool!" Sam agrees.

"*Qué cul,*" José echoes.

They wave at Tía Lola, who waves back.

"*¡Frío-fríos!*" she calls out. Today she has chosen grape flavor in honor of the new color of the house.

By the time Miguel's mother comes home from work, he and his friends look like they have helped Tía Lola paint the house: their mouths are purple smudges. When they open their mouths to say hello, their tongues are a pinkish purple.

"Okay, what is going on?" Mami asks, glancing from Miguel to Tía Lola. She looks as if she is about to cry, something she has not done in a long time.

Tía Lola speaks up. Don't the colors remind her of the island? *"La casita de tu niñez."* The house where Mami spent her childhood.

Miguel can see his mother's face softening. Her eyes have a faraway look. Suddenly, Mami is shaking her head and trying not to laugh. "Colonel Charlebois is going to throw a fit. Actually, he's going to throw us out."

"El coronel, no hay problema," Tía Lola says, pointing to herself and Miguel and his friends. Miguel's mother looks from face to face as if she doesn't understand. Miguel and his friends nod as if they understand exactly what Tía Lola is up to.

The next afternoon, when Miguel's friends come inside from practice, Tía Lola takes their measurements. She has bought fabric with the money the team has collected and is making them their uniforms.

When it is Miguel's turn, he stands next to the mark that his mother made on the door frame back in January. He is already an inch taller!

"Tía Lola, what are you up to?" the team keeps asking. "Are we going to lose our playing field if Colonel Charlebois takes back his house?"

"*No hay problema,*" Tía Lola keeps saying. Her mouth curls up like a fish hook that has caught a big smile.

"Are you going to work magic on him?" Miguel asks his aunt that night.

"The magic of understanding," Tía Lola says, winking. She can look into a face and see straight to the heart.

She looks into Miguel's eyes and smiles her special smile.

As the house painting continues, several neighbors call. "What's happening to your house?" farmer Tom asks Miguel. "I don't believe I've ever seen a purple house. Is that a New York style or something?"

Their farming neighbors think of New York as a foreign country. Whenever Miguel and his family do something odd, Tom and Becky believe it is due to their having come from "the city."

"I've never seen a purple house in my life," Miguel admits.

"Neither have I," José adds, "and I live in the city!"

"I've seen one!" Juanita speaks up, showing off.

"Where?" Miguel challenges.

"In my imagination." She grins.

Miguel has been trying to imitate Tía Lola, looking for the best in people. He stares straight into Juanita's eyes, but all he can see is his smart-alecky little sister.

One afternoon, soon after José has returned to the city, Miguel is coming down the stairs to join his teammates in the back field. He pauses at the landing. The large window affords a view of the surrounding farms and the quaint New England town beyond.

A silver car Miguel doesn't recognize is coming down the dirt road to their house. Just before arriving at the farmhouse, it turns in to an old logging road at the back of the property. Behind a clump of ash trees, the car stops and the door opens.

Later, as he stands to bat, Miguel can make out a glint of silver among the trees. Who could it be? he wonders. He thinks of telling his mother about the stranger, but decides against it. She would probably think an escaped convict was lurking in the woods and not allow the team to practice in the back field anymore.

The next afternoon, Miguel watches from behind the curtain as the same silver car he saw in the woods yesterday comes slowly up the drive. His friends have already left after their baseball practice, and his mother is not home from work yet. He can hear Tía Lola's sewing machine humming away upstairs.

"Who is it?" Juanita is standing beside him, holding on to her brother's arm. All her smart-alecky confidence is gone.

"I think it's him—Colonel Charlebois,"

Miguel whispers. Now that the car is so close, he can make out the old man behind the wheel. The hood has a striking ornament: a little silver batter, crouched, ready to swing. "I'm going to pretend no one is home," Miguel adds.

But Colonel Charlebois doesn't come up to the door. He sits in his car, gazing up at the purple-and-white house for a few minutes, and then he drives away. Later that day, a letter appears in the mailbox. "Unless the house is back to its original white by the end of the month, you are welcome to move out."

"*Welcome* to move out?" Miguel repeats. He wrote ¡BIENVENIDA! to his Tía Lola when she moved in. It doesn't sound right to *welcome* someone to move out.

"We've got three weeks to paint the house back or move," their mother says in a teary voice at dinner. "I'm disappointed, too," she admits to Tía Lola. After all, she really loves the new color. That flaking white paint made the place look so blah and run-down. "But still, I don't want to have to move again," Mami sighs.

Tía Lola pats her niece's hand. There is something else they can try first.

"What's that?" her niece asks.

They can invite *el coronel* over on Saturday.

"But that's the day of our big game," Miguel reminds his aunt. They'll be playing against another local team from the next county over.

Tía Lola winks. She knows. *"Pero tengo un plan."* She has a plan. Miguel should tell his friends to come a little early so they can change.

"Change what?" Miguel's mother asks. "Change the color of the house?"

Tía Lola shakes her head. Change a hard heart. She'll need more grape juice from the store.

The day dawns sunny and warm. The cloudless sky stretches on and on and on, endlessly blue with the glint of an airplane, like a needle sewing a tiny tear in it. Every tree seems filled to capacity with dark green rustling leaves. On the neighboring farms, the corn is as tall as the boys who play baseball in the fallow field nearby. Tía Lola's garden looks like one of Papi's palettes. But now, after living in the country for seven months, Miguel has his own new names for colors: zucchini green, squash yellow, chili-pepper red, raspberry crimson. The eggplants are as

purple as the newly painted house. It is the full
~~of summer. In a few weeks, up in the mountains,~~
the maples will begin to turn.

Miguel's friends and their parents arrive
early. The boys head upstairs behind Tía Lola
and Rudy. Their parents stay downstairs, drink-
ing grape smoothies and talking about how
their gardens are doing. At last, the silver car
rolls into the driveway.

Slowly, Colonel Charlebois climbs out. He
stands, a cane in one hand, looking up at the
house. One quarter of the house is purple. The
other three-quarters is still white. Which color
will the whole house end up being?

Miguel looks down at the old man from an
upstairs window. Suddenly, he feels a sense of
panic. What if Tía Lola's plan doesn't work? He
doesn't want to move from the house that has
finally become a home to him.

He feels his aunt's hand on his shoulder. *"No
hay problema, Miguelito,"* she reassures him as if
she can read his thoughts even without looking
into his eyes.

* * *

Colonel Charlebois is still staring up at the house when the front door opens. Out file nine boys in purple-and-white-striped uniforms and purple baseball caps. They look as if the house itself has sprouted them! Miguel leads the way, a baseball in his hand. Behind them, Tía Lola and Rudy each hold the corner of a pennant that reads: CHARLIE'S BOYS.

Colonel Charlebois gazes at each boy. It is difficult to tell what is going through his mind. Suddenly, he drops his cane on the front lawn and calls out, "Let's play ball!" He stands, wobbly and waiting and smiling. Miguel looks into the old man's eyes and sees a boy, legs apart, body bent forward, a gloved hand held out in front of him.

He lifts his arm and throws the ball at that young boy—and the old man catches it.

Chapter Eight

▼▼▼

Mami's Birthday Party

Mami's birthday party is planned as a small surprise party with a few friends—not unlike
Miguel's birthday back in March.

But soon it turns into a block party that will
be like the ones they used to have in New York.
Except that here in Vermont, there's no such
thing as a simple block. You have neighbors who
have neighbors who have neighbors, and before
you know it, you have a whole county coming
over to your house for your "small surprise party."

There is one other reason why the party
keeps growing that cannot be blamed on Vermont. Tía Lola. She is the friendliest person
Miguel and Juanita have ever known. Tía Lola
speaks with everyone. "To practice my English,"
she explains, though really she just loves people.

After a chat with Reggie, the UPS man

whom months ago she turned away from her door, Tía Lola goes running down the drive after the brown van. "What are you doing on August thirtieth?" she gasps when Reggie finally sees her in his rearview mirror and stops the van.

"Coming over to your house for your niece's party," Reggie replies. "What else?"

Melrose, the town clerk, says the same thing when Tía Lola asks him. And Ernestine, who runs the seamstress shop, and Johnny, who has the car garage, and Petey, who owns the pet shop, and the three waitresses at Rudy's Restaurant, Sandy, Shauna, and Dawn, and Shauna's husband and Dawn's sister and Sandy's partner, who has a best friend....

In less than two weeks, over seventy people will be descending on the house.

"We've got to plan Mami's party, Tía Lola," Miguel keeps reminding his aunt.

But Tía Lola seems unfazed. She stands in front of the house, her head cocked, looking at her masterpiece. The painting is finally finished. The house is completely purple with a salmon-pink trim. "Maybe...just maybe," Tía Lola wonders out loud, "turquoise with hot pink would work better?"

"About the party," Miguel tries again. "We've got to plan, Tía Lola."

"*¿Tú sabes lo que dicen de los planes?*" Tía Lola says, winking. Does he know what they say about plans? Make them, but be prepared to break them!

"Yeah, I know," Miguel agrees. "Like when we invited ten people and now we've got over seventy."

"*¡Exactamente!*" Tía Lola smiles as if she has had nothing to do with it.

On Saturday morning, while Mami putters downstairs, Tía Lola finally calls a secret planning session in her bedroom. She is wearing her purple Charlie's Boys baseball cap atop her high *moño* and carrying a clipboard in her hand as if she were assigning positions to the team.

"*Diez y siete . . . treinta y ocho . . . setenta y cinco,*" she counts. Seventeen…thirty-eight…seventy-five. Suddenly, her head jerks up. They have seventy-five guests coming to Mami's party! They can't fit that many people in the living room!

"I was trying to tell you," Miguel sighs, folding

his arms and giving his aunt a pointed look.

"I know! I know!" Juanita is waving her hand in the air as if she were still in school and had to ask for permission to talk. "Why don't we have the party in the back field?"

"*¡Muy buena idea!*" Tía Lola says, checking that item off the list on her clipboard.

Miguel brings up another problem. "How are we going to cook for so many people? Mami will notice if we start making all this food in the house."

"*Déjame pensar un momentico,*" Tía Lola says. She needs to think a moment.

When Tía Lola thinks, you can see her thinking. Her painted-on eyebrows move slowly toward the center of her face in a thinker's scowl. And just when you think they'll run into each other and become one brow, she jumps up and says, "Aha!" and some Great Idea pops out of her mouth.

This time, nothing pops out of her mouth but a heavy sigh. Nothing pops out of Juanita's mouth or Miguel's mouth, either. They can't figure this problem out.

The phone rings downstairs. Their mother answers. "Oh, hello, Rudy. Let me get her.... Tía Lola!" Mami calls up the stairs.

Miguel, Juanita, and Tía Lola look at each other and cry out, "Aha!"

"I think maybe your aunt and Rudy are becoming very fond of each other," their mother notes to Miguel and Juanita a few days later.

"Is that so?" Miguel says, trying to look surprised.

"She's over there all the time. Maybe Tía Lola will get married after all." Their mother smiles as if she has planned this all along. "Why not? Poor Rudy's been widowed for five years. And Tía Lola, *bueno*, she could do with some good company."

Miguel remembers that his mother once told him that Tía Lola is very sensitive about the subject of marriage. "Mami, why didn't Tía Lola ever get married?"

A sad, wistful look comes over her face. "Remember how I told you my mother died when I was only three? Well, my mami had a younger sister, Tía Lola. When Mami died, Tía Lola took care of me. Maybe Tía Lola was too busy being my mother to find a husband."

This is a surprise to Miguel and Juanita. You

can be a mother without really being *the* mother. You can be a family even if your parents are no longer married.

At last count, seventy-seven people are coming tomorrow. Miguel and Juanita sorely wish they could add one more person to the list of guests.

"You have to remember," the wished-for number seventy-eight reminds them that evening on the phone, "it's your *mother's* birthday, not yours."

"But it won't be the same without you, Papi," Miguel says, lowering his voice.

His mother is having a pre-birthday massage in the living room from her friend Stargazer. Stargazer looks like a hippie to Miguel and Juanita with her long, flowered skirts and natural-fiber tunics, her curly hair and dangly earrings. But Stargazer says she is no longer a hippie but an Irish-Armenian-Native-American with her moon in Cancer. You can't get Stargazer started or you'll ruin Mami's massages with too much conversation.

"I don't see why you can't come," Juanita tells her father. She is on the upstairs extension.

"I'll be there," Papi says. "Really. Just look up,

and you'll see a brush stroke of white in the sky, and that's me, nearby."

"Titanium white?" Juanita guesses in a little voice from her end.

"*Sí, mi amor,*" Papi says. His voice is as small as hers.

But to Miguel, Papi's promise sounds silly. Kid stuff. Like wishing on stars. He is now the captain of a baseball team. He has helped plan a whole surprise party that his mother doesn't know about. He is too grown-up to believe wishes have their own way of coming true.

That night, they tell Tía Lola how sad it makes them feel every time there's a family occasion and their papi—or mami—isn't there.

"You don't ever have to lose anyone you really love," she tells them. "They stay with you in your heart."

That might be so, but it still hurts not to have Papi around.

To brighten things up, Tía Lola brings up the party tomorrow. "I just invited number seventy-eight today."

"Tía Lola!" both Miguel and Juanita cry out.

"But this could not be avoided," Tía Lola explains. "El Rudy's son—"

"No, Tía Lola!" Miguel and Juanita insist.

"This son has a business," Tía Lola continues. "He puts up tents for weddings and parties."

Miguel and Juanita are still shaking their heads when they hear the first raindrops falling on the leaves of the locust trees outside the window.

Early the next morning, Miguel sits up in bed and looks out. The rain is coming down hard as if the leaves all need a good scrubbing before they take on their fall colors. After so much planning, Mami's party will be ruined! Perhaps Papi's hand slipped when he tried to paint only one brush stroke in the sky?

When Miguel goes down to the kitchen, Tía Lola is busy preparing Mami's birthday breakfast. Juanita stands just inside the door, gazing out at the curtain of rain. Two teardrops join the trillion raindrops falling on the ground.

"Don't worry," Tía Lola reassures them. "Everything will be fine."

Just then, their mother enters the room.

"What is going to be fine?" she asks, looking from one to the other.

"Your birthday breakfast," Tía Lola says quickly in Spanish. She sets down a plate of Mami's favorite, fried onions over mashed plantains, which Rudy special-ordered from his distributor in Boston. "*Feliz cumpleaños*," she sings. Miguel and Juanita join in.

"What a wonderful surprise!" their mother cries. Miguel and Juanita look at each other, thinking of the much bigger *sorpresa* that awaits her.

"Our special present comes later," Tía Lola explains, nodding at Miguel and Juanita. They have decided that after the surprise party, they will drive up to their mother's favorite spot in the Green Mountains.

"I don't need another present," their mother says, blinking back happy tears. "This is already so special!"

"The only thing is the rain," Miguel notes. "We ordered a nice day for your birthday." He tries to sound lighthearted, but he can't hide his disappointment.

"I got exactly the day I wanted," his mother replies. "I love rainy days. I wished for one for my birthday."

Miguel and Juanita look at each other, surprised. Then they both glance at Tía Lola, who winks as if she already knew that along with onions and plantains, their mother wanted a rainy day on her birthday.

A little while later, Stargazer stops by. She needs Linda's advice on a display she is setting up in her store for a new line of incense. Behind Mami's back as they go out the door, Stargazer gives Miguel and Juanita the V for Victory sign. Their plan is working out.

As soon as they drive away, the house goes into full gear. Plates are set out. Forks and spoons are laid in baskets. Napkins are stacked in leaning towers. Where are the balloons?

At about ten o'clock, a van pulls in at the purple house on Charlebois Lane. The driver dashes toward the front door in the driving rain. He has a vaguely familiar wide smile and rumpled hair. He wears sneakers and a red bow tie that makes his whole face look like a gift tied with a ribbon. "I got a delivery here for you," he tells Miguel. "Where do you want it?"

"Bring it right in," Miguel says, hurrying away.

"It's too big to bring right in," the man calls after him, but Miguel is already halfway down the hall and doesn't hear. Soon Rudy will arrive with the tasty pastries and dishes Tía Lola has been cooking over at the restaurant. At noon, the guests will start streaming in. Half an hour later, Stargazer will return with their mother. Miguel and Juanita are hurrying here and there, pushing furniture against the wall to make room. With the rain continuing, they have decided to move the party indoors.

"We need Tía Lola's help to move the couch," Miguel tells Juanita.

"Tía Lola!" they both call out. "TÍA LOLA!"

But Tía Lola cannot hear them. She is standing in the back field in the rain, helping the bow-tied man and his three workmen set up the large white tent.

Looking out from the window at the landing, Juanita sees three white peaks above the maple trees. She calls out to Miguel, "Look, it must be Rudy's son!"

They won't have to cram the party indoors after all! Thank goodness for the seventy-eighth guest, even if that guest has not turned out to be their papi.

* * *

Cars are coming down the driveway and driving onto the back field. Neighbors park and step out, squealing, into puddles, carrying gifts and umbrellas. They stand inside the white tent, waiting and visiting with each other. It is the end of the summer. There is talk of what kind of a winter to expect in the months to come.

Finally, over the sound of the rain, they hear a car approaching.

"Get ready!" Tía Lola calls out. A sudden silence falls inside the tent.

Miguel and Juanita look around to make sure everything is in place. Under one of the butterfly piñatas, Rudy and Tía Lola are filling up the last of the purple and pink balloons. Colonel Charlebois, wearing his new purple-and-white-striped baseball uniform instead of his old olive-green army uniform, keeps refilling the popcorn bowl, which Miguel's team keeps emptying. Their neighbors Tom and Becky are crouched on either side of a lamb wearing a pink bow with a gift tag attached. Juanita's friends have finished arranging the presents in a pyramid at the center of the tent. At the far end, Reggie is conferring with Mrs. Prouty about which CDs to play on her portable player. Melrose and Petey tie down the last of the tent flaps.

Have they really made so many friends in just eight months? It seems the whole county has gathered together. How they wish their father were here for this big fiesta.

Just beyond the tent, the car door opens. Their mother steps out, a look of shock on her face. "Surprise!" everyone shouts. And then Tía Lola and Rudy release their balloons with HAPPY BIRTHDAY written across them in big white letters.

Looking up, Miguel and Juanita get their own surprise. Above all their heads stretches the canvas tent, like a broad white (titanium!) brush stroke, keeping them dry as their mother's birthday rain falls steadily outside.

Chapter Nine

▼▼▼

The Best Place in the World

As the last guests drive off, the rain stops. The clouds part and become pieces of litter in the sky that the wind sweeps away. The sunset will be glorious.

Juanita and Miguel, their mother, and Tía Lola pile into the car. They pass the last house in town and drive up the winding mountain road. The air grows cooler. Here and there, red leaves glow on the maple trees.

They sit on an outcrop of rock that overlooks the whole valley. Across the lake and behind the Adirondacks, the sun is setting. The sky fills with splashes of red and gold and purple. It looks like their father's painting *Three Happy Days in Nueva York*.

Then one or two stars begin to show.

~~For a moment, this seems the most beautiful~~ place in the world.

"Thank you," Miguel's mother whispers as if the sunset has been arranged just for her birthday.

"*Muchísimas gracias,*" Tía Lola agrees, bowing her head toward the flashing rays. "Thank you very much." The beauty of the world is an everyday gift. All you need, Tía Lola is always telling them, is to reach out and receive it.

"Now for your last present," Tía Lola says to her niece. "Do you remember how when you were a little girl, I would always tell you a special story on your birthday?"

Miguel and Juanita's mother nods as if she were that little girl again. "It's been a long time," she says, a faraway look in her eyes.

"A long time," Tía Lola agrees. "Today I will tell you that same story but in English."

"*¡Ay, qué bueno!*" Their mother kisses her aunt. "It's so important to me, Tía Lola, that you came to Vermont and learned English so you remain connected to us. And so important," she goes on, kissing Miguel and Juanita, "that you hear Tía Lola's stories so you can always stay connected to your past."

"Speaking of the past...," Tía Lola says, hurrying her story along. The sun is sinking behind the mountains and a chilly wind is coming up.

The wind blows softly through the darkening trees. The leaves make a sh-sh-sh sound as if they are quieting a noisy crowd.

You might not believe this, Tía Lola begins, but once all of the world was warm as summer.

Flowers bloomed and birds sang and the weather was perfect all year round.

And our little island was no exception.

"What about Vermont?" Juanita wants to know.

"And Vermont was no exception," Tía Lola continues.

But people, being people, thought that things were better somewhere else.

Maybe there was more summer farther north? Maybe the sun was brighter down south? Maybe the birds sang prettier songs somewhere else?

So they set out for other places to see what they were missing.

Miguel looks up at the starry sky. *If I see a falling star…* He begins his old magic-wishing game. But it's no use. Some things, like his parents' divorce, he just has to learn to accept.

He wonders if things are better on other planets, other stars. What Tía Lola has said about people is true of him, too. When he is in New York with his father, he misses his mother and new friends. But once he is back again in Vermont, he longs to be with his father and his old friends. It's hard to know what is home anymore.

Maybe it would be better to live on some other planet and be some other boy?

Tía Lola's voice brings him back down to earth and to her story.

People were on the move all over Mamá Earth. No place was exactly as wonderful as the people had imagined it would be, so they kept wandering around.

Some of these people arrived on an island in the middle of a warm blue ocean.

"This is better than where we were before," they said, and they decided to stay.

So was that their home? Juanita wonders. She herself isn't sure anymore where she is from. Both her mami and her papi came from the Dominican Republic. She was born in New York and lived there all her life until eight months ago, when they moved to Vermont. So is she from Vermont now?

Back at the house, her dolls are falling asleep in the boxes that Papi has cut and painted into elaborate cradles. Juanita always keeps them in the same place. When Mami or Tía Lola moves them, Juanita gets upset. Her dolls will feel lost if they wake up and find themselves in a new place, she tries to explain. "Is that the way you feel, *amorcito?*" her mother asks, touching her face softly. Because Juanita's mother is a psychologist, Juanita has to be careful what she says about her dolls because her mother always thinks she is really talking about herself.

But this time, her mother is right. Like her

dolls, Juanita feels lost when she thinks of all the places she is from.

Maybe she will never know where she really, *really* belongs.

Tía Lola continues with her story, her voice like warm waves of sound lapping against their ears.

News spread that there was a place where people stayed put.

That must be the better place, everyone thought, or why would anyone want to stay?

So everyone started to settle there—everyone— and it was a very little island.

Soon the island began to complain. "I just can't hold all these people up!" she cried. "Help me, Papá Sky. Help me, Hermano Sun, Hermana Wind, Amigo Cloud."

And so Father Sky cleared his throat and thundered. Brother Sun beamed down scorching heat. Friend Cloud sent down torrents of rain. Sister Wind blew on the ocean and drove huge waves toward the shore, which smashed down all the houses.

As soon as the rains relented and the seas calmed

*and the sun shone, people began to go back to where
they had come from.*

*The island was quiet again. The birds began to
sing the prettiest songs. The flowers grew bright and
tall. It was as peaceful as it had been before the first
people got there.*

As she listens to the story, Miguel and Juanita's
mother is growing younger and younger by the
minute. She is going back to birthdays past,
when she was a little girl in the Dominican Republic and Tía Lola would tell her this story.
Little Linda would be so proud of having such a
beautiful island as her home, where the birds
sang the prettiest songs and the houses were
purple and pink and yellow and turquoise blue
as if to match the many flowers that bloomed all
year round.

Suddenly, she feels the chilly night air around
her. Years and years have gone by. She is now the
mother of a little girl not much older than she
was when she first heard this story. The mother
of a boy not much younger than she was when
she first came to this country. She puts her arms
around her children and draws them close.

* * *

Tía Lola's voice threads through all their thoughts as she continues with her story.

The people went back to the places they had come from. They were happy again. Home was not such a bad place after all.

But after a day or two or three, they began to doubt themselves. They began to think of going back to where they had last come from.

And so, one night when all the people were suspended in their dreams, Mamá Earth and Papá Sky and Hermano Sun and Hermana Wind and Amigo Cloud had a secret meeting.

"People will always be people," Mamá Earth reminded them. She came up with a plan. "Why don't we make sure every place has something wrong and something right with it? Then people will realize that every place has its good and its not-so-good side."

"Fine idea, Mamá Earth," Papá Sky said, smiling his starry smile.

So they drew up a list of the not-so-good things that could happen. They listed earthquakes and monsoons, blizzards and heat waves, volcanoes and

*terrible hailstorms and driving rain, endless winters
and long mud seasons and summers as hot as something coming to a boil in a bubbling pot.*

*Then all the places on the earth had to pick their
own bad weather.*

*Since the island had worked so hard holding so
many people, she alone was allowed to keep her perfect summer weather all year round. But she was
such a little island, she couldn't use up so much good
luck by herself. So she offered to share this gift with
the other islands in her part of the world.*

*But just in case people would all want to move to
that part of the earth again, the lucky islands decided:
"Let's each take a little bit of bad weather. Let's have
a few heavy rains every year, and a sprinkle of snow
on our highest mountains, and a volcano going off
now and then, and the occasional earthquake or
cyclone or hurricane. That way people will come for
vacation, but not be tempted to stay."*

Suddenly, Tía Lola's voice falls silent. She is
remembering her beloved island. Even with its
occasional tremors and bad cyclones, it is the
place she loves the most. No matter how far she
travels or how long she stays away, she always

wants to go back home to watch the wild parrots fly and the palm trees sway.

Many nights, when the darkness falls and the lights come on and twinkle in the far-off houses, Tía Lola looks up and makes a wish on a Vermont star.

Before the year is out, may I go back to my island home again!

"Tía Lola?" her niece is asking. "What happened to my birthday story?"

"It was taking a little rest," Tía Lola explains. "It has a long way to travel from Spanish to English, from the Dominican Republic to Vermont."

She takes several deep breaths before she goes on.

"Where was I?" Tía Lola says. Her voice is full of energy again.

"You were saying that each island chose a little bit of bad weather," Miguel speaks up. "That way, people would come for vacation, but not be tempted to stay."

"Ah, yes." Tía Lola nods. "Not be tempted to stay...."

And so, when the weather gets cold every-where else, she continues, people from all over the world flock to the Caribbean islands for a vacation. And while they are there, the earth will shake a little or the sun will hide behind a cloud and it will rain for a day, or a volcano will blow a puff of smoke into the sky.

And though the people will be rested and warm, they will think, this is nice, but I'm ready to go home.

"Is that a true story?" Juanita wants to know. She is happy that everyone feels at home at last.

"All good stories are true," Tía Lola reminds her, "but this one is especially true because I made it up for your mother's birthday when she was a little girl like you."

"So do you miss the island, Tía Lola?" Miguel asks. "Do you want to go home?"

"Of course I miss the island," Tía Lola tells them. "But I wouldn't want to miss being here with all of you."

They sit quietly on the rock, looking down at the lights of the little town. Suddenly, Miguel feels happy to be sitting on planet Earth at his mother's favorite spot listening to his aunt's story. Beside him, Juanita is thinking that this is where she really, *really* belongs—next to her brother and mother and aunt.

Mami, too, is thinking that she is so lucky. Although she no longer lives on a beautiful island with her large *familia*, she has found a new home with her children and favorite aunt among a warm *familia* of friends in Vermont.

"Yes, *de verdad*, indeed," Tía Lola is saying. "Home is wherever you are with the people you love. And that is always the best place to be!"

She leans back on the rock and looks up at the sky. She doesn't have to wish on a star tonight.

The sun has long set by the time they rise from the rocks and head back toward the car. The crickets have started up. Far off, a dog, or maybe it's a coyote, barks.

As the car winds its way down the mountain road, Miguel and Juanita sit in the back seat, trying to stay awake. They want to see the first twinkling lights of houses as they come into

town. In the front seat, their aunt and their
mother are talking. "Maybe we can all go back
this winter," Mami is saying. "It would be good
for the kids to meet the family and learn more
about the island."

"I have a great idea," Tía Lola says, lowering
her voice. Now that Miguel and Juanita have
learned so much Spanish, Tía Lola cannot speak
in Spanish if she doesn't want them to understand. Vague, whispery sounds drift to the back
seat as their aunt plans the next surprise treat for
the family.

What could it be? Miguel and Juanita wonder.
They want to lean forward and eavesdrop, but
their bodies feel heavier and heavier.... They are
falling deeper and deeper into sleep...dreaming
of their father painting white tents in the
sky...their mother and Tía Lola flying like parrots south to an island full of purple houses and
swaying palms....

Sometime later, the car rolls to a stop, a door
opens, another one closes. Hands stir them
awake and sweet, familiar voices call out to
them, "Miguel, Juanita, *despiértense. Ya llegamos
a casa.*"

Wake up. We're already home.

Chapter Ten

▼▼▼

La Ñapa

Miguel looks down from his window seat on the plane. The Dominican Republic spreads below him like an enormous emerald-green carpet edged with beaches of snow-white sand. A few hours ago, the ground was a blurry gray. It is hard to believe it is December, that in two days it will be Christmas.

Beside him, in the middle seat, Tía Lola is going through some last-minute tips on island customs. "Americans shake hands," she is saying. "But Dominicans prefer a kiss."

In the aisle seat, Juanita is following the lesson intently. "Is that why you're always kissing us, Tía Lola?"

"Do I kiss you that much?" Tía Lola asks them.

Miguel nods so that Tía Lola will not ask him if he is listening. He is watching the lush green fields coming closer and closer. Tiny trees are becoming life-size, and antlike shapes are turning into real people.

As for Tía Lola's kissing, Juanita is right. Tía Lola kisses them when they come in the house as well as when they go out. She kisses them when they go to bed at night and when they get up in the morning. If she wants to thank them or say she is sorry or congratulate them for helping her clean the house, Tía Lola kisses them as well. Suddenly, Miguel feels worried. He is about to encounter a whole island of people who like kissing as much as his aunt.

"If you go to the market," Tía Lola is saying, "and you buy a dozen mangos, don't forget to ask for your *ñapa*."

"What's that?" Juanita asks.

"A *ñapa* is the little bit more that comes at the end. You buy a sack of oranges, and you ask for your *ñapa*, and you get one more orange or maybe a guava or a cashew or a *caramelo*. You eat your *flan*, and ask for your *ñapa*, and you get another little serving. Let's say a family has seven children, then another one is born. That last one is called the *ñapa*."

"So am I the *ñapa* in the family?" Juanita

wants to know. After all, she is her parents' only other child after Miguel.

"I don't know if it works when there are only two." Tía Lola frowns. "What do you think, Linda?" she asks her niece.

Across the aisle in her seat, Miguel and Juanita's mother looks up from her novel. "I think you should all fasten your seat belts. We're landing."

The plane touches the ground with a little bump like a hiccup. The passengers clap. Looking out the window, Miguel can see men sitting in luggage carts, waiting for their arrival. Just beyond the chain-link fence an old man rides a donkey with a sack of what might be mangos. It's like seeing the modern age and the old days all in one. This is the first time Miguel has ever been to the island his parents both came from. What will it be like?

Suddenly, he wishes he had paid more attention to Tía Lola's lessons all the way down from Vermont.

As they enter the terminal, a band strikes up a merengue. Everyone starts to dance, including

Tía Lola and Mami and Juanita. Miguel is glad none of his friends live here so he doesn't have to feel embarrassed.

They stand on a long line waiting for their turn. Some of the people have red passports. Theirs are blue. "Why?" Juanita asks her mother.

"Because we're American citizens. The Dominicans have red."

Juanita feels proud that she has an American passport, though she wishes that Americans had chosen red since that is her favorite color.

The official in his glass booth checks their passports, peering at Miguel and then at Juanita. *"No parecen americanos,"* he tells their mother. They don't look like Americans.

"We *are* Americans!" Miguel pipes up. He wonders what makes him a real American. Because he was born in New York—unlike his parents, who were both born in the Dominican Republic? Because he speaks English? Because his favorite baseball team is the Yankees? Because he still likes hot dogs more than *arroz con habichuelas*?

In fact, when Miguel glances around, he looks more like these Dominicans holding red passports than he does like any of his classmates back in Vermont.

Miguel remembers part of Tía Lola's lesson on the plane. Maybe the way to prove he is an American is to act like one. He smiles at the official, then reaches up and shakes his hand.

When their suitcases come, six men rush forward to help them, even though all their bags have little wheels.

"*No gracias,*" Miguel keeps saying. But as he is explaining about the wheels to one man, another comes and puts Miguel's suitcase on top of his head like a basket of fruit. "Hey!" Miguel calls out. "That's my suitcase."

"No problem!" the man calls over his shoulder in English as he leads the way through the terminal.

"Let him," their mother says. She explains, "Life is so hard here. It's good to help somebody earn a living."

But even if life is hard, people seem to be having a good time. Inside the main terminal, everyone is visiting with one another. You can't tell where one family ends and another one begins. A group of little girls dressed up in the frilliest party dresses and boys wearing suits that

make them look like tiny waiters are eating
pastelitos out of a greasy paper bag. The Three
Kings are pictured in a billboard whose pieces
suddenly shift and become a man in a cowboy
hat, smoking a cigarette.

"*Feliz Navidad,*" everyone wishes each other.
Merry Christmas.

But how can it be Christmas, Miguel thinks,
when the day is as sunny and warm as a midsummer day in Vermont?

"*¡Ahí están!*" Tía Lola cries out. There they are!

Miguel sees a crowd of relatives standing on
the sidewalk outside the terminal. He is surprised they look so normal. He half expected to
shake hands with uncles with six fingers and
ciguapa aunts wearing braces on their feet. But
his relatives have the same noses, mouths, eyes,
ears, and skin color as Tía Lola and Mami,
although put together in slightly different com-
binations so that each one looks like a different
person.

As Tía Lola and Mami rush forward to kiss
their nieces and cousins and nephews, Miguel
stands guard beside the bags that the porters

have piled beside him. Some of these bags are packed full with presents for all his cousins. There is nothing for Juanita or himself. Their mother has already explained that the trip will be their Christmas gift. Back in Vermont, Miguel thought this was a great idea. All his friends were jealous. "You can go to the beach! You can go snorkeling and fishing! Maybe you'll even get to meet Sammy Sosa or Pedro Martínez!"

But now, standing alone with Juanita, watching these strangers hugging and kissing, Miguel wonders if this trip is such a great Christmas gift after all. His father is back in New York. None of his friends are here. He can't ask for a new video game or a glove since this trip cost a lot.

"*Vengan a saludar.*" Tía Lola is calling them. Come and say hello.

"*Hola, hola, hola,*" Miguel says over and over. In the space of a few minutes, he has acquired a dozen cousins, four aunts, seven uncles. His family has grown into a *familia* a mile long. How is he supposed to remember so many names?

A young boy about his age steps forward. He is wearing a blue baseball cap with a strange insignia on it. Miguel remembers that his mother asked him to pick something out for a young cousin who loves to play baseball and knows some English. "*Me llamo Ángel,*" he says. My name is Ángel. "You play baseball?"

Miguel nods, smiling. Things are looking up. With so many cousins, there are bound to be some he will like. And certainly there are enough cousins to make up two teams and still have some cousins left over to watch them play ball.

Everything is strange and interesting. They drive into the city past row upon row of wooden market stands. At one stand, coconuts are piled up for sale. At another, pieces of meat and long strings of squirming crabs hang from rods. The smells of cooking food and spices and hot sea air and green vegetation waft into the car. The sea matches the turquoise of the sky, and the houses are painted yellow and turquoise and purple and mint green and pink, and the palm trees are like spraying fountains at the ends of tall, slender trunks.

At traffic lights, skinny boys dressed in rags come forward with scraps of cloth to clean the windows. Miguel can't stop staring. "Don't they have parents?" he asks his mother.

"A lot of them don't," Mami sighs. "They live on the streets."

Miguel has seen street people in New York, and it always makes him feel sad and spooky to think someone doesn't have a real home. But all those street people were grownups. These kids are his own age. He feels suddenly very lucky just riding in the back seat of an old Chevy, squeezed between two cousins, with his mother, his little sister, and his aunt all talking at the same time.

At his aunt's house, they sit down to lunch, which is the biggest meal of the day. Miguel has never seen so many dishes of different foods. Every time he finishes, some more *arroz* and *habichuelas* and *puerco asado* and *ensalada de aguacates* are piled on his plate. Rice and beans and roast pig and avocado salad—it's like a *ñapa* that will not quit! The meal lasts for over two hours, the uncles and aunts eating and telling stories and eating some more. When the meal is finally over, everyone stands up, gives each other a kiss, and disappears. "Where did they all go?" Miguel asks Tía Lola.

"*La siesta*," she explains. "To bed to take a nap."

Only babies take naps, Miguel is thinking.

"How can they be sleepy when it's not time to go to bed?" Juanita asks.

"We have a different sense of time," Tía Lola explains. "If someone tells you to meet them at four, it means any time between four and five. We don't live by the clock. Remember the story I told you....We live by the sun and the sea, and we love surprises. Have you noticed?" She winks.

Looking at her radiant face and dancing eyes, Miguel thinks, This is the happiest I've seen Tía Lola in a long time!

Miguel tries to rest in the bedroom he is sharing with Ángel and his brothers. He has begun to worry that Tía Lola is actually planning to stay on the island when they have to return to Vermont. She seems so happy here, speaking Spanish all the time, exchanging stories, fitting right in with everyone else. But if she does stay, Miguel and Juanita and their mother will have no one to tell them wonderful stories. No one to make *frío-fríos* in the summer or sew his baseball uniforms. No one to think up surprises all the time.

This trip has been a bad idea! Once Tía Lola is back on her beloved island, there is no way she will want to return to Vermont.

Around him, he can hear his cousins snoring away, enjoying their siestas. He will never be able to sleep in the middle of the day—especially now that he is worried about Tía Lola.

As he lies there, he hears the pounding of the sea not far away. It seems to be singing Christmas carols to him.

"*Navidad, Navidad,*" the waves sing as Miguel drifts off....

The next evening, the whole extended *familia* gathers together for *Noche Buena,* Christmas Eve. Mami and Tía Lola pile the gifts they have brought under a plastic tree on the patio. Later, Santa Claus will be coming from the North Pole to distribute them among the cousins.

"When is he coming? When is he coming?" the littlest cousins keep asking.

"After you eat your dinner," Tía Lola replies. She is dressed up tonight with gold hoops in her ears and a bright red dress in honor of the occasion. Her beauty mark is on her right cheek again. Sometimes it seems Tía Lola forgets and the beauty mark appears on her left cheek or on her upper lip. Sometimes it doesn't appear at all.

More and more relatives arrive, and there is more kissing and hugging. Several girl cousins recite poems, and everybody claps. One uncle takes Miguel aside to show him the little bone spur next to his pinkie. "My sixth finger!" he brags. His aunts gossip, exclaiming over how big Little Linda has gotten. Miguel wonders if dinner will ever be served. It isn't that he's hungry, but he wants dinner to be over so that presents will be given out. He has figured out a way to get one more gift from Santa Claus.

"When is dinner, *Tía?*" he asks the aunt who is Ángel's mother. It turns out to be the most flattering thing he can say. "This boy is a joy to have in the house," his aunt tells Miguel's mother. "He's a good eater. He's polite. He shakes hands like an Englishman and says, 'Excuse me' when he interrupts." Ángel's mother is looking at Ángel as if to say, *You should learn from your perfect cousin.*

Miguel glances over at his mother, who gives

him her you-and-I-know-better grin. He grins
back.

The plates are cleared away. The uncles push
back their chairs and light up their cigars. Then
the doorbell rings.

Standing before them is Santa Claus. He looks
different from the American Santa Claus—much
more slender, his skin soft brown, his eyes dark and
lively. But he still wears a white beard and a bright
red suit with a thick black belt and shiny boots.

"*Santicló! Santicló!*" The littlest cousins give a
shout and rush forward to make their wishes
known.

When it is Ángel's turn, he unfolds a list from
his shirt pocket and begins to read. "*Un bate, un
guante, una pelota de* —"

"That's enough, Ángel," his mother calls out.
"Remember. Be polite. Ask for only one thing."

Out of Santa Claus's bag come the very bat
and glove and ball that Miguel picked out for his
cousin at the Wal-Mart in Vermont!

When all his cousins have received their
gifts, Miguel steps forward. "My turn," he says.

"Hey, there, my polite and wonderful son,"

his mother calls out. "Remember, you and Juanita already got this trip."

Santa Claus looks at him with dark, dancing eyes. "Yes, Miguel. You already got your gift."

"But I got it in Vermont, and now I'm in the D.R. And my Tía Lola says that here you can ask for a *ñapa*, a little bit more, after you've gotten what you asked for."

Santa looks thoughtful. "Your aunt has a point. I do owe you a *ñapa*, dear boy."

Miguel is grinning. He has been planning this joke on Santa all evening!

But Santa is taking him quite seriously. "Tell me, then, what is it you want?"

Now that his opportunity has come, Miguel cannot think of what to ask for. He really has plenty of video games, and his worn glove is good enough. The vacation itself is turning out to be fun. The day after tomorrow, they will fly to New York, so he and Juanita can spend the rest of the week with their father and old friends. On New Year's Eve, they'll go on a special outing to see all the department store windows Papi decorated for Christmas.

As Santa draws him close, Miguel notices the flash of gold hoops in Santa's pierced ears! Come to think of it, there is something else he really wants.

"Thank you, Santa, for the great trip," he begins. "But just one thing. When it's over, I want Tía Lola to come back home with us."

Santa winks. "I'll see what I can do."

As Miguel turns to go, Santa catches him by the arm. "You are forgetting something," Santa reminds Miguel.

"*Feliz Navidad*," Miguel says. "Merry Christmas!" Then he reaches up and plants a kiss right on the beauty mark on Santa's cheek.

A Word About the Spanish
(Una palabra sobre el español)

In reading about Tía Lola, some of you who know Spanish might wonder if Tía Lola is really speaking Spanish. After all, you know the word in Spanish for a sweater is *abrigo*, not *suéter*. You might never have heard of a *burén* or a *ciguapa* or a potion called *guayuyo*. Or you might have learned that the correct way to say "my son" is *mi hijo*, not *mi'jo*.

First, I want to reassure you that Tía Lola is indeed speaking Spanish. But just as there are many variations in the ways we speak English, people in the Spanish-speaking world have different ways of speaking Spanish. Spaniards are known for lisping their *c*'s and for priding themselves on their "pure" Spanish. We in the Caribbean swallow our *s*'s and elide two-word phrases so they sound like one word (*mi'jo* for *mi hijo*). And we borrow English words—for example, "sweater" becomes *suéter* and "mop" becomes *mope*. In the Dominican Republic, we have our very own words for certain things. We call kites *chichiguas* instead of *cometas*, as they are known in Spain; bananas, *guineo*; and buses, *guaguas*.

So if you know Spanish and wonder sometimes about Tía Lola's Spanish, just remember, she's got her own special *dominicano* she's speaking.

As for those of you who might not know any Spanish at all, I've tried always, *siempre*, to translate each phrase or word right after the Spanish, so that in reading about Tía Lola, you (like Miguel and Juanita) might learn a little bit of Spanish, *un poquito de español*, from her.

Who knows? Maybe one day, someone who speaks only Spanish will move in next door and paint the house purple and offer you a *frío-frío*! And you'll know enough to say, "*Sí, muchas gracias*." Or you might visit a Spanish-speaking country and be able to try out the words you learned in this book.

Speaking of *gracias*, I have a special thank-you to give to my cousin, *mi prima*, Lyn in the Dominican Republic. Often in writing this book, I had to double-check with her about the Spanish. Although I originally came from the Dominican Republic to the United States, I've lived many, many years in English. So every once in a while, I forget how to say a word in Spanish. But I've never forgotten how to say thank you to those special people who help me write my books. "¡*Gracias*, Lyn!"

Julia Alvarez grew up in the Dominican Republic, surrounded by a large family with many aunts. She immigrated to this country at the age of ten with her parents, a watershed experience that she says made her into a writer. She is the author of the Knopf picture book *The Secret Footprints* and many books for adults, including *How the García Girls Lost Their Accents*, *In the Time of the Butterflies*, *¡Yo!*, and *In the Name of Salomé*. She is a writer-in-residence at Middlebury College and lives with her husband, Bill Eichner, in Vermont, but visits the Dominican Republic often, to spend time with her aunts and cousins who still live there.